Dear Reader,

If you thought there were no more Oz books after the original fourteen by L. Frank Baum, do we have a marvelous treat in store for you. Ruth Plumly Thompson, named the new Royal Historian of Oz after Baum's death, continued the series for nineteen volumes. And we will be reviving these wonderful books, which have been out of print and unattainable anywhere for almost twenty years.

Readers who are familiar with these books swear that they are just as much fun as the originals. Thompson brought to Oz an extra spice of charming humor and an added richness of imagination. Her whimsical use of language and deftness of characterization make her books a joy to read—for adults and children alike.

If this is your first journey into Oz, let us welcome you to one of the most beloved fantasy worlds ever created. And once you cross the borders, beware—you may never want to leave.

Happy Reading,
Judy-Lynn and Lester del Rey

THE WONDERFUL OZ BOOKS
Now Published by Del Rey Books

By L. Frank Baum

#1 The Wizard of Oz
#2 The Land of Oz
#3 Ozma of Oz
#4 Dorothy and the Wizard in Oz
#5 The Road to Oz
#6 The Emerald City of Oz
#7 The Patchwork Girl of Oz
#8 Tik-Tok of Oz
#9 The Scarecrow of Oz
#10 Rinkitink in Oz
#11 The Lost Princess of Oz
#12 The Tin Woodsman of Oz
#13 The Magic of Oz
#14 Glinda of Oz

By Ruth Plumly Thompson

#15 The Royal Book of Oz
#16 Kabumpo in Oz
#17 The Cowardly Lion of Oz
#18 Grampa in Oz
#19 The Lost King of Oz
#20 The Hungry Tiger of Oz
#21 The Gnome King of Oz
#22 The Giant Horse of Oz
#23 Jack Pumpkinhead of Oz
*#24 The Yellow Knight of Oz
*#25 Pirates in Oz
*#26 The Purple Prince of Oz

* Forthcoming

Jack Pumpkinhead of OZ

by
Ruth Plumly Thompson
Founded on and continuing the Famous Oz Stories

by
L. Frank Baum
"Royal Historian of Oz"

with illustrations by

John R. Neill

A Del Rey Book
Ballantine Books • New York

Library of Congress Catalog Card Number: 85-90576

ISBN: 0-345-32360-2

Cover design by Georgia Morrissey
Cover illustration by Michael Herring
Text design by Gene Siegel

Manufactured in the United States of America

First Ballantine Books Edition: October 1985

10 9 8 7 6 5 4 3 2 1

This book is
affectionately dedicated
to my aunt Joe.

Ruth Plumly Thompson

IMPASSABLE

The MARVELO⟨

GILLIKIN

COODGOD

CORUMBIA SAMM CORABIA
Quick City
Parashuter
(Subterranea-U)
Flathead Mt.
Mist Valley
Skeezer
Reeta
Spiders
Ozwoz

Gamet
Kiama
Party
PATCH
Double
Up
Jack
Pott

Great
Gillikin
Forest

Forest
of
Gugu

Soap
Slide
Suds

Dangerous
Passage
Bewilderness

Buttonwood
KIMBALOO
Gillikin
Hooper
Laughing
Willows
Somewhere
Inland
Sea
Backwoods
Scooters

Wish
Way
Sun Top Mt.
Tune Town

Catty
Corners
Blankenburg
Dr. Nikidik
Mombi

Pokes
Candy Giant
Fix
Twigs
Kite Is.
Equinots
Hidden
Valley
Shadow Mt.

Winkie
River
Road
Ice town
Book
ville
Serpent
Tree
Marsh
Land
Loonville

WINKIE

Perhaps City
Maybe Mts.
Play City
Monday Mt.
Witch of
the West

Squirrel
King
Wish
Way
Black
Forest
Mt. Much
Tree of
Whutter Wee
Village of
Field Mice

Tin
Woodman's
Castle

Jack
Pumpkinhead
EM⟨
C

Merry-Go-Round
Mts.
Scarecrows
Tower
Wise Acres
Lake
Quad

Ugu
Great
Orchard
Thi
Rolling
Prairie
River

Herku

COUNTRY

Bear
Center
Scare City
Chimneyville
Utensil
Bunbury
Bunnybu

Tottenhots
Flutterbudgets

Winkie
Woods
Bottles
Up &
Down
Water
fall
Mr. Yoop
Hoppers
Horners
Rigmarole
Town

Swing
City
Big Er
(Loxo)
Little Eno

Bourne
Land of
the Barons
Red

Big Top
Mt.
Baffleburg
Lollypop Village
Carrot
Mt.

QUADLING
Ruby Imps
Cavern
Twinlet Town

South
Mt.
Dark
Forest

Truth
Pond
Posties

YIPS

**Based on the
Original Map
drawn by
Professor
H.M.WOGGLEBUG,T.E.
Revised
in accordance with
the
Royal Histories
of
OZ**

**JAMES E. HAFF
Delineavit**

N
W E
S

Winkie River

Trick River

DEADLY DESERT

Spin R.

GREAT   S

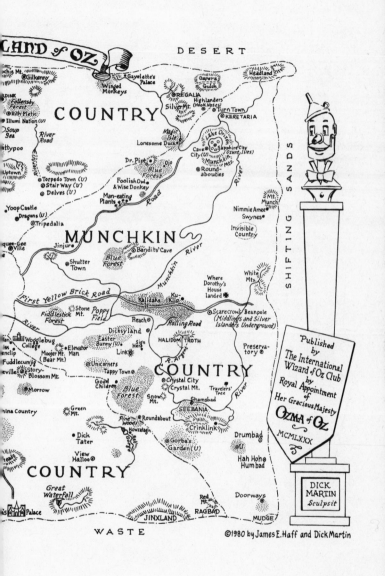

DESERT

LAND OF OZ

Gilkenny
chie Mt.
DINK
Follensby
Forest
Rith Metic
Soup
Sea
River
Road
attypoo
Uptown
Torpedo Town (U)
Stair Way (U)
Delves (U)
Yoop Castle
Dragons (U)
Tripedalia
que-Gee
Ville
Jinjur
Shutter
Town

COUNTRY

Winged
Monkeys

Gayelette's
Palace

Gabera
Gulch
Headland

REGALIA
Silver Mt.

Highlanders
(Hook Noses)
Turn Town
KERETARIA

Magic
Isle
Lonesome Duck

Dr. Pipt
Ojo
Blue
Forest

Foolish Owl
& Wise Donkey
Man-eating
Plants

Lake
Cave
City (U)
Sapphire City
(Ozure Isles)
Munchkin
Mts.
Round-
abouties

Mt.
Munch
Nimmie Amee
Swynes
Invisible
Country

MUNCHKIN

Bandits' Cave
Blue
Forest

Munchkin River

White
Mts.

Where
Dorothy's
House
landed

First Yellow Brick Road

Stone
Mt.
Poppy
Field
Kalidahs
Ku-
Klip
Scarecrow's Beanpole
(Middlings and Silver
Islanders Underground)
Fiddlestick
Forest
River
Reach
Rolling Road
Dicksland
Easter
Bunny (U)
Sign
Here
Link
HALIDOM TROTH
Preservatory
Wogglebug
College
Moojer Mt.
(Bear Mt.)
Elevator
Man
ss
enclip
Fuddlecumjig
Unicorners
COUNTRY
R. Argent
Tappy Town
Travelers
River
eville
Story-
Blossom Mt.
Good
Children
Crystal City
Crystal Mt.
Travelers'
Tree
Morrow
Blue
Forest
Snow
Mt.
Shamsbad
SEEBANIA
nina Country
Green
Mt.
Pine
Woods
Roundabout
Dick
Tater
Howsatagn
Crinklink
Drumbad
View
Halloo
Gorba's
Garden (U)
U.
Hah Hoh
Humbad

COUNTRY

Great
Waterfall
s Int Palace
Red
Mt.
RAGBAD
Doorways

JINXLAND

MUDGE

WASTE

©1980 by James E. Haff and Dick Martin

SHIFTING SANDS

Published
by
The International
Wizard of Oz Club
by
Royal Appointment
of
Her Gracious Majesty
OZMA of OZ
MCMLXXX

DICK
MARTIN
Sculpsit

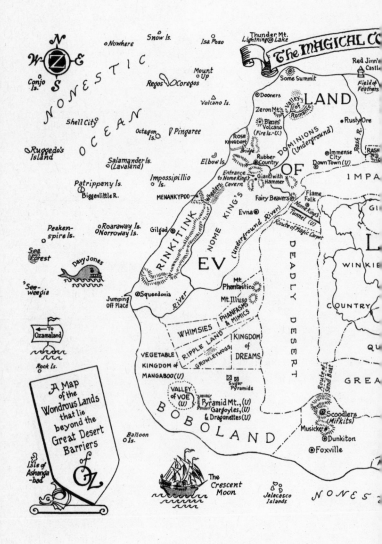

RIES surrounding OZ

Isle of Dork

Roly-Rogues Is.

The Sea Fairies

NONESTIC OCEAN

North Mts.

KINGDOM OF IX
City of Ix
Nole

NOLAND

Aquareine's Palace (Undersea)

Roly-Rogues

Isle of Phreex

DESERT

SKAMPAVIA

Valley of Lost Things

Valley of Toy Animals

MERRY -LAND

Valley of Clowns

COUNTRY

Valley of Pussy-cats

Valley of Bonbons

Palace of Romance

ND OF

MUNCHKIN

Valley of Dolls

RIVER

Valley of Babies

Isle of Mifkets

EMERALD CITY

SHIFTING SANDS

Heelers

Pirate Is.

OZ

COUNTRY

LOLAND HILAND

Lo Hie

The Enchanted
Forest of Lurla
HEG
AURIEL SPOR DAWNA
Twi
PLENTA
Isle of Yew

COUNTRY

Island of Civilized Monkeys

ORKLAND

ANDY WASTE

KINGDOM OF SCOWLEYOW

Mt. Mern

AURISSAU
Jackdaw's Nest
Fistikins

Groves of Trom

Lerd

VALLEY OF MO

Maple Syrup
Cream
Puffs

Hurr-Ha!

RIBDIL

BILKON

Caves of the Daemons

Bumpy Man

(Phunnyland)

JUNKUM

est of rzee

LAUGHING VALLEY of HOIHAHO

MACVELT

Turvyland (t/) Maetta

Seventon

ABUMBIA

MULGRAVIA

QUOK

To Pessim's Island

King Anko

OCEAN

Based on the Original Map drawn by Professor H. M. WOGGLEBUG, T.E.

James E. Haff
Del.

Dick Martin
Sculp.

©1980 by James E. Haff and Dick Martin

List of Chapters

CHAPTER 1

Peter and the Pirate's Sack

THE RAIN beat heavily on the roof, swirled down the side walks and made tumbling torrents of the gutters. Turning from the window in disgust, Peter dropped his baseball mitt on the library sofa and started glumly toward the stair. No practice to-day, doggone it! Why couldn't it rain on Mondays and be clear on Saturdays for a change? How was he to have the team in trim for the big match if this sort of thing kept up?

Kicking crossly at each step, Peter progressed

1

toward the attic. Not to waste the day, he resolved to have a look at his fishing tackle. The thought of the fishing trip he was soon to take with his grandfather cheered him considerably and by the time he had switched on the attic light and dragged out the old chest where he kept his treasures, he was whistling softly to himself. On top of the chest lay two coarse sacks. They were neatly folded in half and as Peter lifted them off he gave an amused little chuckle.

"I wonder what's happened in Oz lately," mused Peter, sitting down in front of the chest with the sacks on his lap. "I wonder whether Ozma knows what I did with the pirate's gold pieces and whether the Gnome King has got into any more mischief." And thinking of that enchanting and enchanted Kingdom, Peter forgot all about his fishing tackle.

Now many of you may have read or heard of the marvelous Land of Oz, but Peter had really been there; had met the Scarecrow and the wonderful Wizard; had kept the Gnome King from conquering the Emerald City and even discovered a pirate ship full of treasure. The pirate who owned the ship had once been a real pirate, so when Ozma, the little girl ruler of Oz, transported Peter and the treasure back to Philadelphia, two of the bags of gold had been real gold and these bags had come with him. These very sacks that Peter held across his knees had once bulged with gold pieces.

And those of Peter's friends and relations who had sniffed at the story of his amazing journey to Oz never had been able to explain them away.

Peter's grandfather, with whom the little boy lived, had not tried to explain them, for Peter's grandfather was old enough to believe almost anything. So he and Peter had spent one bag of gold very gaily on a trip to the coast, on motorcycles for Peter and his best friends, on a club house for the team, on canoes and some more things, too. The other bag they had changed into United States dollars and put into the bank, so that Peter might go to college and other important places when he was grown. And now, with the rain drumming steadily on the roof, Peter fell to dreaming again of Oz, of its curious Kings and castles, its wizards and witches and magic transformations. Could it have been two years ago that he and the Gnome King escaped from Runaway Island?

"I wish," sighed Peter, giving the top sack a little shake, "I wish I could go back to Oz sometime. Hello! What's this?" In the corner of the top sack he felt something hard and round and thrusting in his hand drew out a thin shiny piece of gold. "Why, here's one we didn't find," chuckled Peter, holding it up to the light. "It's not so large as the others. I believe I'll keep it for a lucky piece." Resting his head against a small trunk, Peter sank back and was soon lost in pleasant reveries. "Gee whiz!" he breathed at last, flipping the pirate's coin into the air. "It certainly would be great to go to Oz again. I wish I were there right now!" As the gold piece dropped into Peter's palm, Peter himself dropped out of sight. At least, he was no longer in the attic, or in Philadelphia either, for that matter. He was, to be perfectly truthful, standing before a small yellow cottage in the middle of a pumpkin field, and the whole trip, reflected Peter, staring around a bit wildly, had taken no longer than one puff and swallow. A drop such as this was enough to make a body puff and swallow several times, so he did. Then, having regained a little of his composure, he looked uncertainly at the yellow house.

It was shaped like an enormous hollowed out pumpkin, but had several windows and a front door, so Peter walked boldly up the steps and knocked twice. He could hear footsteps running about inside and presently a head was thrust out the second story window.

"Who's there?" asked the owner of the house, staring down curiously.

"It's me, er—er it's I!" Peter, remembering his grammar corrected himself quickly.

At this, the owner of the house, in order to have a better look at his visitor, leaned so far out the window that Peter gave a sharp cry.

"Oh look out!" he called warningly, for the man's head seemed ready to fall off, was falling off, in fact.

"I am looking out," it called cheerfully, as it turned over and over in the air. "That's just the trouble! Catch my head will you?" And next minute Peter found himself clasping a large pumpkin head in both arms.

"Did you say your name was Cy?" asked the head, staring up inquiringly. "Well carry me indoors, Cy. You'll find my body around somewheres."

"This must be Oz," choked Peter, with an excited little gasp and, kicking open the door, he hurried into the cottage. A tall awkward body sprawled on the floor and there was certainly something familiar about the hollow eyes staring so pleasantly into his own.

"My body has fallen down the stairs," observed the pumpkin head calmly. "It should have waited for me, for nobody should be without a head." Peter agreed heartily with this last statement and, setting the head on the table, he pulled the awkward figure to its feet and then, standing on a chair, pressed the head carefully on the wooden peg that served for a neck.

"Why it's Jack Pumpkinhead!" he cried delightedly. "Didn't I meet you in Ozma's palace two years ago? Don't you remember me?"

Jack looked doubtfully down at the little boy. "I'm afraid that I don't," he answered seriously. "You see, I have had several new heads since then, and am not very good at remembering."

"Never mind. I remember you!" Peter smiled

"WHO'S THERE?" ASKED THE OWNER OF THE HOUSE, STARING OUT
CURIOUSLY.

7

kindly at the awkward fellow and, squeezing his wooden fingers, went on. "My name is Peter and—"

"I thought you said your name was Cy," objected Jack in a puzzled voice.

"Oh no I didn't," explained Peter, a little vexed at the pumpkin head's stupidity. "I said it's I at the door."

"Cy at the door and Peter in the house. How dreadfully confusing," mumbled Jack, putting one hand to his head to see if it was on straight. "Have you a different name for every place you go?"

"Oh call me Peter!" exclaimed the little boy impatiently, "and if you'll just tell me the way to the Emerald City I'll not bother you any more. I'm anxious to see Ozma and Dorothy again."

"Are you a friend of Ozma's?" interrupted Jack in high excitement. "Well, I'll do anything for a friend of Ozma's. Ozma is my father!" Running to the door Jack clattered down the steps, beckoning for Peter to follow him.

"Father!" cried Peter, with a little burst of laughter, and then realizing one could not expect too much sense from a pumpkin head, he hurried out of the cottage. The pirate's sack still hung over his arm and, tossing it gaily over one shoulder, Peter stepped quickly after Jack, and clapped him on his shoulder.

"By the way, how did you reach Oz?" Picking his way carefully between the rows of pumpkins,

Jack paused and turned his head with both hands so he could look back at Peter. Briefly Peter told him of finding the last coin in the pirate's sack, how he had wished to be in Oz and suddenly found himself standing before the yellow cottage. "It must have been a magic coin," muttered Jack Pumpkinhead, starting on again. "I tell you," he gave an excited skip, "that gold coin was a piece of change. You wished to come to Oz for a change and here you are!"

"Yes," agreed Peter slowly. "But where is the gold piece?"

"You can't have the change and the gold piece too," reproved Jack, wagging his wooden finger, "and you'd rather have the change, now wouldn't you?" Peter nodded and glanced sharply at Jack. His head seemed to be working better. Jack returned Peter's look with a long, steady stare. "Do you know," he said, stepping deliberately over a high fence onto a gold paved highway, "You remind me more and more of my dear father."

"Your dear father," exploded Peter, sitting down on the top rail of the fence. "I thought a while ago you told me that Princess Ozma was your father."

"She is," answered Jack, marching calmly along the highway.

"But Ozma's a girl," shouted Peter indignantly, catching up with Jack. "How could a

10

girl be your father and how could I remind you of Ozma?"

"Ozma was not always a girl," explained Jack mysteriously. "Once Ozma was a boy like you. I see you have never heard my strange story," finished Jack in a hurt voice—looking reproachfully down at Peter. Though Peter had met Jack Pumpkinhead at Ozma's palace he had to admit that he knew nothing of his interesting history. So, as they sauntered slowly along the highway, Jack told how Ozma, as a baby had been stolen by Mombi, the witch and transformed into a boy named Tip. For nearly nine years, Tip had lived in Mombi's hut, entirely ignorant of the fact that he was the real ruler of Oz. It was to scare Mombi that Tip had first manufactured the Pumpkinhead Man. Jack's wooden arms and legs had been skillfully carved from strong saplings. His body, made of a tough piece of bark, was pinned together with wooden pegs. A larger peg served Jack for a neck and a carved pumpkin made his head. With some old clothes he found in Mombi's attic, Tip had dressed the queer figure and stood him in the bend of the road to scare the old witch on her return from a visit to the crooked wizard's.

"Well, was Mombi scared?" inquired Peter, looking admiringly at Jack's jointed wrists and ankles and thinking what a smart boy Ozma must have been.

"At first," admitted Jack slowly. "At first!

Then, wishing to try out some of the magic she had traded with the wizard she sprinkled me with the powder of life and immediately I came to life and have been alive ever since," he finished modestly.

"But what happened to Tip?" begged Peter, for he felt that the most exciting part of the story was to come.

"Well," continued Jack with a solemn shake of his head, "as Mombi threatened to turn Tip to a marble statue, we both ran away that night, taking the powder of life with us. Next morning Tip found a saw-horse standing in a wood and, sprinkling it with some of the powder, brought it to life as Mombi had done me. On this strange steed we reached the Emerald City and helped the Scarecrow, who was then Emperor, escape from Jinjur's army of girls, who had captured the capitol. After many curious adventures we reached the palace of Glinda, the Good Sorceress of the South. We begged her to help us restore the Scarecrow to his throne, but Glinda, by referring to her magic records, discovered that Ozma was the rightful ruler of the Kingdom. Returning to the Emerald City, Glinda forced Mombi to disenchant Tip, Tip became Ozma and Ozma, as you well know, has been our gracious little sovereign ever since."

"What a shame," breathed Peter kicking at a stone, "I should think she'd much rather have stayed a boy."

"So should I," agreed Jack, "but as I am only a pumpkin head my opinion is probably of no value. I certainly have no reason to complain," he went on cheerfully. "Ozma gave me the fine cottage which you saw this morning and I spend all my time growing new heads. Before one pumpkin spoils, I quickly carve myself another and have had dozens of heads in my day, which makes me a personage, even in Oz. This head I'm now wearing will last quite a long time for it's still a bit green."

"Well, it looks all right," said Peter, smiling up at Jack.

"Do you think so?" Jack's carved grin seemed to grow even broader at Peter's polite remark. "If it were not for my joints, I'd be as good as anyone," he confided, tapping his chest proudly. "But walking wears out my joints so I never walk far at a time."

"Is it far to the Emerald City?" Shading his eyes Peter blinked down the gay gold highway and then turned rather anxiously to his cheerful

companion. He certainly did not want good
natured Jack to wear out any joints on his
account.

"No distance at all," retorted Jack, with a
stiff wave ahead. "Around that bend the houses
and trees will be green, for we will be on the
outskirts of the capitol, and from there it is but
a step to the palace." At Jack's word Peter gave
a satisfied little sigh. It was all coming back—
his geozify. Oz! How well he remembered that
great oblong Kingdom, divided into four smaller
kingdoms, with the Emerald City in the exact
center. In the Eastern Winkie Country of Oz,
the houses, fences, fruit and flowers were all
yellow; in the Southern Quadling Country they
were red. In the Northlands of the Gillikens
they were purple and in the Western Kingdom
of the Munchkins they were blue. From the
daffodils in all the fields and the round yellow
farm houses, Peter knew they were in the
Winkie Country, but at the next turning they
should find the green trees and parks surrounding the loveliest city in Oz.

Thinking of this enchanting spot, its gay and
jolly inhabitants and the welcome he was sure
to find in the palace, Peter quickened his steps,
reaching the bend of the road far ahead of Jack.
But instead of flowering gardens and green
parkways the highway ended abruptly in a high
red brick wall. There was a small black door
in the wall. In red letters on this door were
two words—"Enter Here." Peter was staring

uncertainly at these directions when Jack caught up with him.

"Well Cy! What now?" he demanded merrily. "See, I remembered you were Cy, at the door. Ha, ha! Ho, ho, ho!"

"Oh do try to be sensible," begged Peter in an annoyed voice. "Can't you see that this wall is red? We must be in the Quadling Country, Jack. You've come the wrong way and we're lost! Now, the question is whether to go back the way we came or go through this door and try to find a short cut to the Emerald City."

"I was afraid this head was not quite ripe enough," mumbled Jack in a worried voice. "Perhaps if we go through this door and turn straight North we'll find the Emerald City just as quickly as if we turn back."

"Perhaps," echoed Peter doubtfully. Then, as he was beginning to feel an overpowering curiosity as to what might be on the other side of the wall, he opened the black door and stepped through.

CHAPTER 2

The Chimney Villains

"NOW I'm Santy Claus," mumbled Jack, feeling around for his head. Both he and Peter had stepped off into space and tumbled together down a long dark passageway. "We've fallen down a chimney," continued Jack, finding his head and settling it firmly on his shoulders. "I must say this is a great way to enter a city."

"It is a grate," said Peter, with a little groan, for he was sitting astride a pair of iron fire

16

dogs, "but how do you know it's a city?" Fortunately there was no fire burning in the grate and, picking up the pirate's sack, Peter stepped out into a large red square. Jack had to bend almost double to get out at all and as he straightened up a sign hanging on the outside of the chimney caught his attention.

"Please shut the grate after you," directed the sign. Being an obliging fellow, Jack pulled the handle at the right and a sliding black screen completely closed off the opening. Dusting the soot from his frayed coat, Jack joined Peter.

"Nothing but chimneys," marvelled the little boy with a low whistle. "I've often seen houses without chimneys but never chimneys without houses." The square was simply bristling with chimneys, all red and of every shape, size and description. They seemed to sprout like queer flowers from the red flags that paved the square. Chimneys! Chimneys! Chimneys! So close together there was scarcely space to walk. "Who could possibly live here?" said Peter, with a scornful sniff.

"Whee! Whee—ee! We do!" A hundred high voices answered his question. They seemed to issue from the chimneys themselves, and as Jack and Peter peered anxiously upward strange smoky figures began to spiral out of the chimney tops and float in a dark mass over their heads. They looked like evil genii or goblins who had long been imprisoned in magic bottles. Their

shapes and faces changed constantly and as a whole horde of them dropped downward, Peter stepped closer to Jack. "They're only smoke," he explained reassuringly.

"Yes, dear Peter," quavered Jack, "but smoke is most injurious to pumpkins! Oh my head! My poor poor head!" Peter had no time to sympathize with Jack, for at that moment a crowd of Smokies surrounded them. Their eyes were spite-red sparks and, snatching at Peter and Jack with their long shadowy arms, they began to hiss and puff threateningly.

"Can you curl?" demanded one, snapping his eyes close to Peter. "Can you curl, and do a double spiral? Can you make soot and smoulder?"

"No! No! No!" coughed Peter, snatching out his handkerchief and waving it wildly about his head. "Go away! Go away. You're making me all black."

"Ha, Ha, Ha!" shrieked a great smoky giant. "That's the color you should be. This is Chimneyville, but wait till you see our Soot Sooty down below. Come to our Sooty and see how black and beautiful you will become."

"We won't," cried Jack Pumpkinhead defiantly, "we won't come or become. If this is Chimneyville, then you are Chimney-villains. Go away you black monsters. We refuse to visit your old Sooty. Go away, go away. You're smoking my beautiful head." Trying to cover his head with his arms, Jack backed against a chimney, but his words only seemed to infuriate the Smokies. Swelling with rage, they surged forward.

"Smoke 'em up! Smoke 'em out! Throw 'em down the chimneys!" they sputtered. "Now then, boys, all together!" While Peter and Jack struck out left and right, the grim gray specters tried to lift them into the air. But there was no strength in their vapory arms and with little shrieks and hisses they pressed closer and closer.

"Run!" panted Peter, who was almost suffocated. The smoke did not affect Jack and, taking Peter's hand, he tried to pull the little boy along. But the air was now so thick with their pursuers they could hardly see at all and bumped and crashed into chimneys at every turn. The last bump flung them headlong, and for a moment they lay perfectly still, while the Chimney-villains swept screaming overhead. It was dark as midnight, for the Smokies had all run together into a great suffocating cloud. Even the tiny sparks that were their eyes had gone out, and in utter and awful darkness Peter finally stumbled to his feet. Coughing and sputtering and with tears pouring down both cheeks, he felt in his pocket for another handkerchief, and as he did his fingers closed over a small candle end. Immediately a bright idea struck Peter, and with a gasp he felt around for Jack's head. Pulling the stout stem in the top he lifted out the piece Jack had cut

20

when he hollowed out the pumpkin. Striking a match he lit the candle end, spilled in a few drops of candle grease and set the candle erect. Then replacing the top of Jack's head he jerked him to his feet.

"What have you done?" faltered the Pumpkinhead in a faint voice. "My head feels very light, dear Peter, but I seem to see much better."

"So do I," choked the little boy, muffling his nose in his coat sleeve, "we can both see better. Come on, you're lit up and my Jack o' Lantern now!" The bobbing light in the pumpkin's head seemed to puzzle their enemies, but Peter, guided by the cheery glow, pushed bravely through the clouds and crowds of them. The smoke still stung his eyes and throat, but he kept dodging chimney after chimney, and finally pausing to rest against an especially broad one, discovered a slide like the one they had come through in the first place. Jerking it open Peter pulled Jack into the grate and closed the slide. There was another slide at the back of the chimney place and as the Smokies poured against the first slide Peter opened the second and stepped out into a quiet little wood.

"A great way in and a great way out," observed Jack, following Peter quickly and slamming the slide after him.

"And a great way from everywhere," puffed Peter, dropping down on the nearest tree stump and staring resentfully up at the red wall. It looked the same from this side as from the other. Not a chimney showed, nor one puff of smoke, to warn luckless travellers of the disagreeable citizens of Soot City. It was so great a relief to breathe pure air again and find himself in real daylight that Peter sat for several minutes drinking in the fresh forest breezes and freeing his lungs from the bitter smoke. Then, standing up on the stump, he called Jack and blew out the candle in his pumpkin head. "You certainly saved my life that time," said Peter feelingly. "If you had not lighted me out of there I'd have been a smoked herring by this time. How do you feel yourself, dear Jack?"

"A little light headed," confessed Jack earnestly, "but on the whole, I rather liked it. It seems to me I felt brighter."

"You mean you could think better?" asked Peter, staring hard at Jack, and trying not to laugh.

"Yes," Jack nodded gravely, "so please light me up again dear Peter."

"It might not be good for you," said the little boy doubtfully. "It might make you light headed and giddy. Besides, pumpkins are only lit at night or in the dark and it's quite light out here."

"Oh are they?" Jack looked terribly disappointed. "Well any time you need a lantern, just light me up. Shall we go on to the Emerald City now?"

"Well, we might try to," answered Peter

looking around with lively interest. "Can you walk a little farther? Do your joints feel all right?" Although Jack was much taller than he, Peter felt somehow responsible for the flimsy fellow. It rather flattered him to have Jack so obedient to his wishes and so dependent upon his advice. After examining his joints carefully, Jack decided he might go a bit further, so Peter washed his face in a little stream and at the same time removed the soot from Jack's, and they prepared to continue their journey to the capitol. Taking his direction from the sun, Peter started North through the little wood. From the cardinals and robins, from the red beech and holly trees, he knew he must still be in the Quadling Country and when he saw a small red cottage in a clearing just ahead, he was sure of it.

Goody Shop, announced a sign, swinging from the crooked roof. "Hurrah!" shouted Peter, breaking into a run. "Maybe I can buy something to eat here. It must be nearly lunch time and I'm starved."

"Oh do be careful," warned Jack, holding to his head with both hands as he dashed hurriedly after Peter, "they may not be the kind of goodies you expect." The shop was dim and dark and behind the red counter sat a prim little old lady in a ruffled gown.

"Good morning!" puffed Peter with a polite bow.

"Our good morning is all gone," said the old

lady, rising stiffly from her tall stool, "but we have a very good afternoon, would you care for that?" She squinted anxiously at Peter. "And will you take it with you or have it sent?"

"Have it sent," advised Jack in a hollow voice for he did not relish the old lady's expression.

"I wanted to buy something good," explained Peter hastily.

"Well why didn't you say so in the beginning," snapped the shop keeper testily. "One minute it's good morning and now it's goodbye. What kind of a goodbye do you want, long, short, fond or sorrowful?" At this strange question, Jack turned his head with both hands and simply stared at the old lady, and Peter himself began to feel terribly confused.

"What kind of goods do you sell here?" he demanded anxiously.

"All the goods," answered the old lady proudly, "but dry goods mostly. Waving toward the shelves, she folded her arms and looked suspiciously at her two customers, while Jack and Peter curiously surveyed her wares.

"Good news! Good advice! Good Intentions! Good Days! Good Night! Good Excuses! Good Riddance!" cried Peter, reading out the labels on the bottles and boxes. "How odd! Good Ideas! Good Tempers! Good Notions! Good Times!"

"Come, come," muttered the old lady, tapping her foot impatiently on the floor, "make up your minds. You may each choose one," she

decided finally, as neither Peter nor Jack seemed able to decide. "Why don't you take a good excuse?" she suggested, turning to Peter. "Boys are always needing good excuses, and a fresh batch has just come in—good ones too!"

"I think I'll take some good advice," announced Jack in a timid voice. "I'm not very bright and it might be useful."

"But haven't you anything good to eat?" sighed Peter. "A good lunch or dinner, even a breakfast would do." With an impatient flounce the old lady reached up on a top shelf and handed Peter a small red box. Then giving Jack a red envelope, she shooed them out of her goody shop.

"I wish I'd taken some good excuses," murmured Peter, as they walked slowly down the crooked path. "This box is too small to hold a good meal of any kind."

"What does it say?" asked Jack inquisitively.

"A good breakfast," answered Peter reading the red label. "Well, even if it's only a biscuit or just one sausage, I'll eat it." Eagerly Peter raised the lid. "Why it's bird seed," he exclaimed angrily, flinging the box with all his force into a red-berry bush. "What a cheat! I've a good notion to go right back and tell her what I think of her."

"But she didn't charge you anything," observed Jack mildly, "and you'll have to admit it is a good breakfast!"

"A good breakfast," roared Peter, glaring indignantly at his loose-jointed companion.

"Well, it is a good breakfast," finished Jack Pumpkinhead apologetically, "for a bird." Peter looked closely at Jack to see whether he was poking fun at him, but quite soberly, Jack was opening his good advice.

"What does yours say?" Crowding closer, Peter read the words on the thin slip of paper and then began to hop up and down with glee.

"Keep your mouth shut," advised the red paper briefly.

"Call that good advice?" sputtered Jack Pumpkinhead, tearing the paper into tiny pieces. "How can I keep my mouth shut when it's carved open? Of all the silly nonsense!"

"But you'll have to admit that keeping your mouth shut is good advice," teased Peter, completely restored to good humor by this joke on Jack.

"Then why don't you take it?" asked Jack stalking stiffly ahead. "Take it and welcome!" Smothering another chuckle, Peter hurried after Jack, reflecting to himself that this Pumpkinhead Man was not nearly so foolish as he appeared to be.

CHAPTER 3

What the Green Tree Said

"WON'T Dorothy and Ozma be surprised when we turn up at the palace?" Taking a running jump, Peter cleared a tree and then hurried back to help Jack Pumpkinhead across.

"I'll be surprised myself," said Jack, stepping solemnly over the log. "Here we are at the end of this wood and no signs of the Emerald City at all. Do you see anything green, Peter?" Peter shook his head, for as far as the eye could

28

reach there was nothing but rocks and sand, tinged with the rusty red of the Quadling Country.

"I see red, nothing but red," sighed the little boy in a depressed voice. "Wait, there's one green tree, though—a fir tree. Why, it's running straight for us. Hey! Look what you're doing! Get off my foot!" Giving the tree a quick shove, Peter sprang backward. But the tree leaned a little further over, and resting its lower branches on his shoulders began to sob heavily.

"I'm very tired," it panted in a weak whisper, "very tired!" It spoke through a hollow in the center of its trunk and its knot eyes stared mournfully into Peter's own.

"Well, you can't lean on me," exclaimed Peter crossly, giving it another push. "I'm tired too! Why I never heard of such a thing," he continued in an indignant voice. "What are you doing, where are you going, why don't you act like a regular tree?" Wrenching the branches from his shoulders, Peter stepped off and eyed it angrily.

"You don't belong in this country anyway," put in Jack accusingly. "You're green and you know it!"

"Hush," muttered the tree, putting a lower branch over its mouth. "I'm a Christmas Tree, looking for last year's ornaments." There were a few gay colored balls still clinging to the top and as Peter, too astonished to make any reply continued to stare, the tree drew closer.

"Are you a Christmas present?" it asked hoarsely. "Are you an ornament?"

"Oh go away!" laughed the little boy, giving it another shove. "Do I look like a Christmas present? And can't you see we're not ornaments?" With a little chuckle, he waved at his companion.

"I could use his head, "murmured the tree, squinting through its branches at Jack. "It's not at all pretty, but it would light up and look real merry. Here you!" With a sudden pounce the tree made for Jack. "Give me your pumpkin head and no nonsense either!" As Jack and Peter both jumped back together, a simply astonishing thing happened. From the end of each branch on the Christmas tree a hand shot out, and with each hand extended it dashed after them.

"See! I trim myself!" it yelled, snapping its fingers hilariously. "Come here you provoking boy. I'll wager you have plenty of stuff in your pockets I could use for presents. Have you a watch or a gold pen knife?" At each question, it made greedy snatches at Peter. "Let me pick your pockets! Give me your head you great jumping-jack!" Ten of its hands just grazed Jack's coat tails.

At first Peter had been rather amused by the Christmas tree, but now, thoroughly alarmed, he clutched Jack's hand and ran so fast that Jack had all he could do to hold on to his head and keep from stumbling. As they continued to

elude it, the determined little tree grew very angry. Hopping up and down on its roots, it seized the ornaments from its top branches and hurled them one after another at the fleeing pair. Three balls and a candy cane crashed to bits on Peter's head, and as he dodged in between two big boulders a silver dinner bell tied with red ribbon hit him sharply between the eyes.

"Gee-whiz!" spluttered the little boy, clapping his hand to his forehead, "this is no fun!" Pulling Jack after him, he squeezed into a narrow crevice between the rocks, but before he did Jack leaned down, picked up the bell and slipped it into his pocket. As the Christmas tree attempted to push its way between the rocks, Peter and Jack pressed against a rough wall at the back. Now it happened that in this wall there was a swinging rock door, and as they both leaned hard against it, the door swung inward and spilled them abruptly into a narrow stone corridor. Next instant the door slammed to, leaving them sitting in surprise and consternation on the rocky floor. They could hear the tree pounding with all its fists against the panels, but a bolt had dropped into place as the door closed, so there seemed little danger of further pursuit.

"I wish we'd stop this falling about," complained Peter, picking himself up a bit wearily. "We're always doing something we don't expect."

"That's because we're in Oz," answered Jack cheerfully, "and at any rate, we have saved my head from the Christmas tree."

Peter felt inclined to remark that saving Jack's head was not so very important, but thinking better of it, he went on in an exasperated tone: "Christmas trees in our country don't chase people nor throw things at them. They stay where they're put."

"Yes," said Jack Pumpkinhead blandly, "I suppose they do, but Oz Christmas trees are more progressive, more up-and-coming." Taking out the silver bell the Christmas Tree had thrown at Peter, Jack held it close to his ear and then swung it slowly to and fro. At its first silver ring Peter, thinking it would rouse the owner of the cave, rushed over to stop Jack, only to collide violently with a tiny black slave who had apparently sprung up from nowhere. He wore a simply enormous turban and carried an immense silver tray. Regaining his balance with great composure, the little black slave set the tray on the floor, folded his arms and with a deep bow melted into thin air.

"It's a dinner!" shouted Peter, dropping on the floor and hungrily snatching off the white napkin that covered the tray. "Well, of all things!"

"Unexpected things, you mean," corrected Jack slyly, "and I notice you don't object to this one."

"Let me see that bell," puffed Peter, reaching

across the tray. It was not very light in the cavern, but even so he could read the inscription on the shining silver surface. "The Red Jinn's dinner bell," said the carved letters mysteriously. "A magic dinner bell," exclaimed Peter delightedly. "This certainly makes up for the bird seed. And did you see that boy dissolve into nothing right before our eyes?" Jack nodded.

"Better eat that dinner before it does the same thing," he advised calmly. As this seemed not at all improbable, Peter made short work of the roast duck, mashed potatoes, hot rolls and apple sauce. He had just finished the last roll, when tray, dishes and silverware vanished suddenly.

"Shall I ring the bell again?" inquired Jack, as Peter stared dazedly at the spot where the tray had been. Although Jack was not constructed for eating, he had thoroughly enjoyed watching Peter.

"No," decided the little boy with a satisfied nod, "I've had enough, and it was good. But I wonder how that Christmas tree got hold of the Red Jinn's dinner bell?"

"Stole it probably," answered Jack, rubbing the bell on his sleeve. "Maybe the old Jinn didn't run fast enough. Anyway it's a regular Christmas present for you, Peter. Whenever you're hungry we'll just ring it." With a pleased chuckle, Jack slipped the bell back into his pocket.

"It certainly will be useful," sighed Peter,

patting his stomach with a contented little sigh. Now that his hunger was satisfied, he felt quite cheerful and adventurous again. "Let's see where this passageway leads," he added, peering round the dark corner at the end of the little corridor.

"Why don't you throw that old sack away?" inquired Jack Pumpkinhead, as they walked slowly along the strange hallway. "What good is it?"

"I don't know," answered Peter, swinging the pirate's sack carelessly to and fro. "I had it when I landed here and it might come in handy to carry things in."

"What kind of things?" asked Jack stupidly. Peter did not bother to answer for they had come suddenly upon a great scowling goblin-head lantern. Under the lantern hung a flashing red sign.

"T—remble!"—directed the sign in big red letters.

"I don't see why we should tremble," said Peter, squinting defiantly up at the goblin lantern. At Peter's words the lantern went out, and whistling through the dark windy corridor came such a succession of wails, sighs and horrid screeches that Peter's heart stood still.

"Are you trembling?" quavered Jack, as the hair raising noise died away. "Not exactly," stuttered Peter, leaning against the wall to steady himself. As the lantern flashed on again, he peered anxiously all around. But there was no one in sight, so putting back his shoulders and taking a deep breath Peter marched bravely forward. "There's nothing to be frightened about," he called reassuringly over his shoulder.

"Well, nothing certainly made enough noise," murmured Jack, straightening his head which had spun round and round at the horrible outcrys. "I wish we were safely out of this, dear Peter." Peter did not say so, but he heartily echoed Jack's wish. As they progressed along the strange corridor the goblin lanterns became more numerous and ugly, and the last turn brought them to a high, red, spiked gate. On every spike there was a frowning scare head, and as the two travellers paused uncertainly, each head stuck out its tongue.

"Boo—OO!" shrieked the heads altogether, so loud and so shrilly that Peter almost took to his heels and Jack, without meaning to at all, sat down. As the little boy hurriedly tugged him to his feet, the red gates swung open.

"Welcome to Scare City!" boomed a horrid voice. "Quake! Shake! Pale and tremble!"

CHAPTER 4

Scary Times in Scare City

O N THE other side of the spiked gate rose
a curious cliff city. There was a great
court in the center surrounded by a mass of
jagged rocks and from the rocks narrow cliff
dwellings had been crudely hewn and cut.
Crooked, carved steps led down into the
courtyard and every rock and inch of wall space
was covered with roughly drawn heads and
frowning faces, while set on stone poles at
regular intervals were hundreds of goblin

lanterns. A bluish green smoke hung in the air and every minute or so it would rise and form into the words "Scare City! Scare City! Scare City!" so that altogether the whole effect was exceedingly grim and unpleasant. So much so, in fact that Peter and Jack turned to flee. But the arm that had pulled them through the gate, held them fast.

"Pause!" commanded a harsh voice. "Pause! Pale and behold the Chief Scarer!" Swallowing hard, Peter took an unwilling look at the gate keeper. He was about six feet tall and his head seemed to be face all round, with eyes on every side and noses that stuck out like spikes in every direction. As Peter, with a little shiver, turned away, he began to speak again. "You!" rumbled the Chief Scarer, pointing a skinny finger at Jack, "are a perfect fright! But you," contemptuously he looked Peter up and down, "you would not even scare a baby. How dare you come here with that soft white pudding face?" Now Peter, as you can well imagine was thoroughly frightened, but the words of the gate keeper made him angry and anger made him bold. Stamping his foot and drawing his face into a terrible scowl, Peter stuck out his tongue.

"Is this better?" he demanded furiously.

"A little! A little!" sighed the Chief Scarer, leaning thoughtfully on his staff. "Could you cross your eyes?"

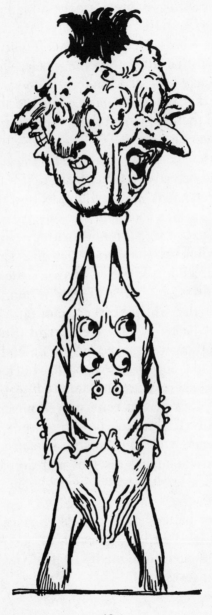

"Don't you do it Peter!" begged Jack. "They might stay that way."

"Well, suit yourself," yawned the Scarer indifferently. "I doubt whether either of you will pass the tests anyway, and if you don't you'll be turned into Fraid Cats, or scared stiff. You're supposed to tremble in the presence of the King, you know, and if you run you'll turn to Fraid Cats and if you scream you'll be scared stiff. Remember, now, I warned you." Lifting a red whistle to his lips, the Chief Scarer blew three sharp blasts and then stepped back into his niche in the rocks.

"Who's afraid?" muttered Peter in a defiant voice. "They can't scare us, can they Jack?" Before Jack could answer, a perfect horde of Scares rushed out of the rock dwellings and began to tumble and leap down the steps into the court. Halfway down, they paused and one with a particularly frightful face bawled impressively; "Tuh-remble, for you are in the presence of the King!" Jack and Peter had no trouble at all in trembling. Jack's knees knocked together so hard that one of the pegs fell out of his joints and his pumpkin head bounced up and down upon its peg. Peter twisted his hands behind him and gritted his teeth to keep from screaming. He felt exactly as he had when he was a small boy and a rough crowd of Hallow'een ghosts and goblins pounced suddenly upon him in his own front yard.

"They're no worse than masqueraders," said

41

Peter pluckily. "Don't run! Don't scream, Jack, no matter what happens."

"What I don't see, won't frighten me," answered Jack, and reaching up with both hands he turned his head so that the back was toward the Scares. Each Scare was different but each one was dreadful. Some had blue faces, some red faces and others green faces but they all had dozens of noses and the result was more than terrifying. Scurrying here and there in between the feet of the Scares, were the Fraid Cats meowing piteously when anyone trod on them. Instead of tails these singular beasts had two heads, one at each end so that it was impossible to tell whether they were coming or going. Swallowing nervously, Peter resolved that whatever happened he would not run and turn into one of these two headed tom cats. When the Scares almost reached the spot where the two travellers stood trembling, the one they called King stepped out on a high flat rock. He had a horn for a nose, a lion's mane, pig eyes, donkey ears and billy goat whiskers.

"Three groans for Harum Scarum the Seventh," shouted his subjects and proceeded to groan most lustily, while Harum Scarum, waving both arms, addressed Peter and Jack in words so long and frightening that the air fairly quivered, and bits of rock, loosened from the walls, rattled down like hail stones.

"What is he saying?" panted Jack, who still had his head turned.

"They're trying to scare us with big words," shouted Peter above the awful din. "Don't move, Jack; whatever you do, don't move."

"But suppose they run over us?" wailed Jack Pumpkinhead dolefully. Peter had thought of this himself and as the Scares, evidently disappointed at not making them run, stopped shouting and prepared to attack, he seized Jack's hand and whispered frantically. "Here they come! Here they come! What shall we do? What *shall* we do?" How Jack, with only a pumpkin head, ever thought of the magic dinner bell Peter often wondered afterward. But he did think of it, and before the Scares had advanced a foot he snatched out the bell and shook it furiously. Instantly the little slave appeared, set a tray before Peter and vanished. And Peter, without delay, seized the silver dishes full of food and hurled them at the oncoming foe.

The astonishment of Harum Scarum and his band was comical to behold. Hit by flying forks, spoons, tumblers, bowls of chicken and mashed potatoes and finally by the silver tray itself, they paused in utmost confusion. Before they could pick up the flying missiles they had disappeared and when, with yells and shouts they started forward again, Jack rang the Jinn's bell a second time and a third time and a fourth time and with never a pause Peter flung dinners and dishes at their heads. But when Jack rang the bell a fifth time, the little slave appeared

44

and, looking reproachfully at Peter, set down only one small bowl of soup. Five dinners in less than five minutes was too much for even a magic dinner bell.

With a gasp of dismay, Peter flung the bowl at Harum Scarum and then snatching the pirate sack from his shoulder swung it defiantly round his head. Nothing could save them now, but at least, decided Peter, he would go down fighting. Jack, too, seemed to realize the hopelessness of their situation and, turning his head, boldly confronted the Scares, doubling up his wooden fists prepared to struggle till he fell. With noodle soup in his goat's beard and fury in his pig eyes, Harum Scarum rushed at Peter. As he did, the pirate sack jerked out of the little boy's hand. The strings had been loosened by Peter's wild swings and now the mouth was open wide. Sailing through the air like a small Zeppelin, it scooped up Harum Scarum, then the ten Scares behind him, then the ten Scares behind them, snapping and swallowing, snapping and swallowing till not a Scare nor a Fraid Cat remained in the courtyard. Then swiftly the sack returned to Peter and quietly collapsed at his feet. There was not a sound in that whole strange city, nor a single Scare in the sack.

"Why didn't you tell me you had a grab bag?" stuttered Jack. "Tie it up quick; do you want it to grab us?" With trembling hands and stiff fingers Peter pulled the cords in the top of the sack, and sinking down in a tired heap leaned his head against the stones. The battle with the Scares and the strange behaviour of the pirate's sack had almost been too much for him. Where in Pete had the Scares gone and how could the sack be empty? Jack equally agitated took several jerky steps up and down and then paused in front of Peter.

"What now?" asked Jack Pumpkinhead inquiringly. "What now?"

"Let's get out of here!" exclaimed Peter, and taking a long breath he jumped to his feet.

"Are we going to take that?" Fearfully Jack pointed to the pirate's sack.

"Of course!" said Peter, trying to speak in a matter of fact voice. "It might help us out again."

"Do you wish to be helped out of sight?" wheezed Jack sarcastically. "Why, it may swallow us any minute that our backs are turned."

"Not if we keep it tied," answered Peter with more confidence than he felt. "We really ought to take it to the Emerald City to show the Wizard. I don't believe even the Wizard has seen a sack like this. It's a trained sack, I suppose. That pirate taught it to swallow his enemies and now it will swallow ours."

"All right, bring it if you must, but don't swing it near me." Straightening his head resignedly, Jack began looking around for the peg that had fallen out of his knee joint. When

Peter had found and replaced the little wooden piece, they hurried quickly to the entrance of the city. The gate keeper had been swallowed with the rest of the Scares and though Jack and Peter pulled and pushed and tugged they could not budge the iron bolts.

"Maybe there's another way," puffed Peter, finally giving up the attempt. Turning from the entrance, they walked round and round the courtyard and climbed wearily up and down the rocks, but could find no break in the wall, nor any way out of the grim City.

The dead silence, now that the Scares were gone, was dreadfully depressing. Thoroughly discouraged, Peter and Jack sat down on a block of granite. Leaning his head against a red pillar, Peter took a last despairing look around. As his eye travelled slowly over the court, a red stone griffin, or what Peter had supposed to be a red stone griffin, rose majestically from the base of a pillar. With a terrific stretch and yawn it opened its eyes, blinked in surprise at Peter and Jack, then raising one claw called gently, "Who? What? Whither? Why?"

CHAPTER 5

Peter Meets the Iffin

"BOY! Pumpkin! Emerald City! Because!"
answered Jack who was extremely
literal.

"If everyone would answer me as sensibly as he does," said the griffin, "I'd talk all
day. So you say you're leaving this place because——"

"Because we hate it," said Peter, looking
steadily at the strange speaker. So many things
had happened in the last hour that Peter felt
only a slight twinge of surprise at the creature's
curious appearance and conversation. "Are you

48

a griffin?" Peter asked, rubbing his forehead wearily. It looked not unlike pictures he had seen of this rare and fabulous monster—being sandy red in color, with a huge lion's body and dragon's claws. Its head, instead of being the usual eagle head, was of rather a doggish nature with a stand-up mane and inquisitive, pointed ears.

"You must be a griffin," repeated Peter, noting the powerful wings starting from the monster's shoulders.

"I am a griffin without the gr—rr," answered the animal, sitting dolefully back on its haunches. "I used to be a real griffin, but since my capture and imprisonment here I've completely lost my gr—rr, which makes me by the process of simple subtraction an Iffin. To while away the hours of my captivity," it went on patiently, "I acquired the habit of thought. I thought and I thought and thinking brought on iffing. I began to if about this and that till I became a philosopher."

"What is a philosopher?" asked Jack suspiciously.

"A philosopher is an Iffin too," rumbled the singular beast, scratching his ear reflectively. "He thinks practically all the time and he says to himself:

"If this and that are really so, then so are that and this;
That being so, 'tis best to go so far, then one can't miss!

49

"Everything hinges on the if," he finished brightly. "See?"

"I'm afraid I don't," said Jack, shaking his head stupidly. "Do you, Peter?"

"Well, I understand about the if," answered the little boy, who could not help grinning at Jack's puzzled expression. "If the Iffin will just show us the way out of Scare City, we'll go and not miss a single thing."

"If it were not for the Scares, I would," wheezed the big beast, peering nervously up at the rocks. "But it's no use; they'll only turn you to Fraid Cats or statues. Besides I'm chained." He lifted one paw to which a heavy chain and padlock were attached. The other end of the chain was fastened to the base of the pillar.

"Say, you must be a sound sleeper," marvelled Jack. "Didn't you hear the big battle? This boy and I have conquered the whole city and Harum Scarum and the Scares are gone—vanished, done for."

"Gone!" cried the Iffin, lashing its tail in astonishment. "How? When? Where?" Jack pointed silently to the sack which Peter still had over one shoulder, and Peter quickly told of their exciting encounter with the citizens of Scare City, of the great usefulness of the Red Jinn's dinner bell and the way the pirate sack had finally swallowed down the whole company of horrors. At Peter's recital, the Iffin's eyes grew rounder and rounder and as he finished

it put up both wings and with short agitated
jumps shrieked:

> "The Scares are gone, then what scare we!
> The Scares are gone, we're free, we're free!

"Loose this chain," it panted, tugging impatiently away from the post. As Peter, now as
excited as the Iffin, looked hurriedly around
for a bar or stone to break the padlock, Jack
stepped forward and warningly held up his
hand.

"Just what do you eat?" asked Jack Pumpkinhead in an anxious voice. "Are you carnivorous?"

> "If an Iffin were carnivorous, would he relish
>   red geraniums?
> I live on flowers, solely, so please get that
>   through your craniums.

"What did you think I ate, little boys?"
finished the Iffin sulkily.

"Well, you never can tell," murmured Jack,
with a worried glance at Peter. "I just wanted
to be sure." Peter chuckled to himself, and
while looking for a spike discovered a gold key
suspended from a nail on one of the red pillars.
Taking the key, he fitted it into the rusty
padlock and after several unsuccessful attempts
it turned and the heavy chain fell with a loud
clank to the red paving stones.

"Do you really eat geraniums?" asked Peter,
as the Iffin sprang away from the post and
rushed in crazy circles around the court yard.

"Of course," it snorted boisterously. "Of course!" Then spreading its wide red wings it soared majestically into the air—up, up and out of sight.

"Why it's gone!" shouted Jack Pumpkinhead indignantly. "There's gratitude for you! Gone and left us without even a claw shake or thank you."

"Maybe it will come back." Kicking aside the chain, Peter strained his eyes to catch a glimpse of the flying monster, but not one speck showed in the murky sky overhead. If Jack and Peter had been blue before, they were navy blue now. With their only means of escape removed they looked blankly at one another, while the goblin lanterns glowed and smoked and the sulphurous air of the cliff city grew more dry and unbearable.

"If I'd only made it promise to help us before I turned the key," sighed Peter regretfully.

"Hah! So you're an Iffin, too." Peering around a pillar, the bright red eyes of the sandy colored beast winked merrily into Peter's. "Just trying out my wings," it explained gruffly, "and they're wonderful!

> "If you don't think so, listen to them swirl
>   and whirl and swish;
> Climb on my back, I'll carry you to any place
>   you wish."

"Will you really," cried Peter, falling joyfully

on the Iffin's neck. "Can you take us to the Emerald City?"

"If you want me to," answered the Iffin, wagging its tail bashfully.

"Have you a name," inquired Jack Pumpkinhead, getting stiffly off the granite block.

"Well," said the Iffin slowly, "I've been here so long I forgot my real name but the Scares called me Snif. I'm not sure I know the way to the Emerald City, but I will fly over the wall into the Land of the Barons and there we can surely find someone to direct us. Since you have freed me from my captors I will serve you faithfully for seven years."

"Hurrah!" shouted Peter, hugging Jack. "I'm not sure I can stay in Oz that long, but I'm certainly glad we fell into this city. Meeting you was worth all the trouble." In reply the Iffin chortled:

> "If you hadn't come, I'd be here yet,
> So I'm glad as a Gluckbird that we met."

"What's a Gluckbird?" asked Jack, straightening his head and looking rather severely at the irrepressible monster.

"If I knew I'd tell you," confided the Iffin, coming close to whisper in Jack's ear. "Let's make ourselves scarce around here," he called boisterously in the next breath.

"Oh let's," agreed Peter, swinging up the

pirate's sack. "You mount first Jack and be sure to hold fast to your head."

"And be sure that bag's shut," added the Iffin, wiggling his nose rapidly. "I've never travelled with a magic sack and though I fly I'm no swallow!"

"Is the dinner bell all right?" asked Peter, tightening the cord of the pirate's sack and helping Jack climb on Snif's back. There was just room for the Pumpkinhead to sit astride in front of the Iffin's wings and Peter settled himself comfortably back of Jack between the mighty pinions. With one last scornful look at the red city, the Iffin rose into air, mounting higher till the goblin lights of Scare City were no larger than fire flys twinkling below.

"Were you a prisoner long?" asked Peter, as Snif flew swiftly over a bright red forest.

"Five years," bellowed the big beast, looking over its shoulder. Flying seemed no effort at all and it talked quite easily as it flew. "The first year," it explained sadly, "I struggled and growled so hard in my efforts to escape that I

completely lost my gu-r-r-r. See!" Clearing its
throat, the Iffin attempted a growl but succeeded
in producing only a faint squeak. "After I lost
my gu-rr," it went on in a melancholy voice,
"I amused myself making up iffish verses, a
habit I fear I shall never recover from."

"I like it," said Peter after a short pause. "It
reminds me of Scraps. She's a live Patchwork
Girl who lives in the Emerald City. Scraps
talks in verses all the time."

"If the Patchwork Girl can talk in rhyme
She must be 'most as smart as I'm."

smiled Snif, with a wink at Jack Pumpkinhead.

"She is," laughed Peter with a reminiscent
chuckle. "I say, there must have been a lot of
travellers from the number of Fraid Cats in
Scare City. Why did they have two heads?"

"So they'd be forced to look at Scares which
ever way they turned," sighed the Iffin. "Every
Scare had his cave full of statues of people who
had come to Scare City by mistake and been
frightened stiff. You were lucky to escape."

"Well," admitted Peter with pardonable
pride, "it's pretty hard to scare the Captain of
a baseball team and Jack is not easily frightened
either."

"So I see, er—saw," observed the Iffin
politely.

"When we reach the Emerald City, Ozma
will find a way to release all of these prisoners

wherever they are," said Peter confidently. "But how did they capture you?"

"I dropped into the city at night," said the Iffin, "and before I saw how bad it was they overpowered and chained me up. They wanted me to stay and devour all travellers and even when I refused they kept me as a curiosity. And that's all I'll be from now on," it wheezed heavily. "I'll never get the taste of sulphur out of my throat, the picture of the Scares out of my mind or be able to growl again. I'm quite all wrong."

"You seem all right to me," said Peter, with a little sigh of content. "Wait till you see the Emerald City. You'll forget all about the Scares and never ever want to leave again, will he Jack?"

"Never," answered Jack, with a solemn nod.

"I have heard the capitol is very lovely," mused the Iffin, "but my home is beautiful, too."

"Where do you live?" inquired Peter. Jack was too busy holding on his head to join in the conversation.

"In the Land of the Barons, among these hills." Pausing in mid air, the Iffin pointed with its claw to the rolling hillside below. Here and there above the trees and on the hill tops lordly castles reared their round, red towers. Flags fluttered from every turret and Peter had to admit that the Land of the Barons looked extremely interesting and gay.

"Are these barons pleasant fellows?" he asked, putting a steadying arm around Jack Pumpkinhead. The Iffin answered in verse:

"If they're good, they're good as pie,
But some are bad and make things fly—even me."

"You mean there are all kinds," mused Peter.

"Yes," said the Iffin. "And they're always fighting, but I don't mind battles. I just fly around till they're over and they're quite interesting to watch."

"I hope we don't land in the middle of a battle," sighed Peter. "And I hope the first Baron we meet is a good fellow and knows the way to the Emerald City."

"If he is, and if he does, we'll be as gay as never was;
And if he's not and if he don't, we'll find a way, swumped if we won't!"

"You use such funny words," sniffed Peter, as the monster circled lower and lower. But the Iffin made no answer this time, for he was looking for a good place to land. Presently he found one, and next instant they dropped gently down into a peaceful valley. As Peter and Jack tumbled off in great excitement, Snif folded his wings and blinking self-consciously murmured, "Well, here we are. Do you like it?"

CHAPTER 6

The Bearded Baron Appears

AFTER Scare City almost any place would have looked beautiful to Jack and Peter, and this quiet valley overgrown with vines and sweet smelling flowers, seemed lovely indeed.

"You're a whiz, Snif," exclaimed the little boy, looking around appreciatively. "Why, you travel faster than an aeroplane. You're even better than one, for you can walk and talk as well as fly."

"Swim, too," grunted the Iffin, panting a

little from the exertion of the journey. "Now if you'll excuse me, I think I'll run along and find some geraniums. They grow wild around here and I'm wild about 'em."

"Don't get lost," begged Jack Pumpkinhead, for this accommodating new steed seemed almost too precious to let out of their sight. "Shall I go with him?" he whispered hurriedly to Peter.

"It might hurt his feelings," said Peter, dropping luxuriously into the long fine grass. "Let's rest till he comes back and then we can hunt up one of these barons and inquire the way to the Emerald City." Rolling over on his back and looking up at the drifting summer clouds, Peter gave a long sigh of content. "Why, this is almost as interesting as my last trip to Oz, Jack—travelling around with you this way and meeting an Iffin, and everything. No matter what happens we're not so badly off for we have a sack to swallow our enemies, a magic dinner bell to supply us with food and an enchanted steed to carry us wherever we wish to go. Gee, I wish some of the fellows were along! I wish my Grandfather had been with us in Scare City. You were great, Jack, to think of that dinner bell!"

"Was I?" Leaning against a tall young beech, Jack beamed down at Peter. "You were great, too," he insisted generously. "I never saw anyone throw so straight and so hard."

"Playing baseball does that," explained Peter,

clasping his arms behind his head. "We'll have to have a game when we reach the capitol. Say look! Here are some wild strawberries." Scooping them up by the handful, Peter began to eat hungrily. "Did you ever see such large ones?"

"The Quadling Country is noted for its red fruits," answered Jack proudly, "its strawberries, apples, cherries and red bananas. Sometimes I wish I were made to enjoy eating," he finished, looking rather wistfully at Peter.

"You do miss a lot," agreed the little boy sympathetically, "but then on the other hand, you never suffer from hunger and could never starve to death. But here comes Snif." Swallowing the last of the strawberries Peter ran to meet the Iffin. Several geraniums still drooped from the corners of his mouth and he was loping along humming cheerfully to himself.

"All aboard for the Emerald City," he called merrily, as he came closer. "That ought to please your long-legged friend, there. He's all board from his neck down, anyway." Smiling at Snif's little joke, Peter picked up the pirate's sack, helped Jack to mount and sprang nimbly up behind him.

"Are we going to fly or walk," he asked curiously.

"Waddle," puffed the Iffin with a droll wink. "I'm so full of geraniums I'd simply sink if I tried to fly, so if you're all ready we'll waddle along."

"I'm afraid waddling won't be at all good for

my head," objected Jack, as the Iffin started off with swinging, uneven strides. Peter laughed as Jack continued to protest against waddling, but the Iffin was too busy practising gu—rrs to pay any attention to the Pumpkinhead.

"It's funny," it muttered between its teeth. "I can say gu-rr but I can't growl it, and until I can growl, I'm no griffin."

"Oh, what do you care," said Peter. "Any old grouch can growl, but not many can fly, swim, waddle and make verses like you do. I'd rather be an Iffin than a griffin, any day."

"That's because you never were either," sighed the big monster with a little shake of his head, and quickening his pace he galloped along so swiftly that Peter and Jack had all they could do to hang on. Once out of the valley, the country spread before them, like a gay and enchanting map. Little patches of shadow lay on the velvety hills, small wooded parks dotted the hollows and many castles were visible in the distance. Beyond, a huge range of red mountains lifted their craggy heads to the sky.

"We'll stop at the first castle," decided the Iffin, jumping without effort a tall timber fence that enclosed one of the parks. Red deer scattered right and left, as the huge monster rushed by and they were progressing finely when, from the center of the park where the trees were thickest, came a sharp, shrill wail.

The Bearded Baron Appears

"Perhaps we'd better try the second castle," panted the Iffin, flattening back his ears:

"If that looks like it sounds, I prefer not to look;
It's either a Snort or a sort of Gazook."

Before Jack could inquire what a Snort or Gazook might be, before the Iffin could even turn, steps came pattering toward them, and out through the trees rushed a tall, trembling old man in a red cloak.

"I am a mess! I am a mess! I am a mess!" he croaked, flinging out both arms desperately.

"Tut! Tut!" reproved the Iffin, putting up his ears. If you don't shout it so loud, maybe no one will find you out. Keep it quiet, I beg of you."

"I am a mess, I am a mess, a mis-erable mesmerizer," insisted the old man, drawing his hand wearily across his brow and leaning heavily against a tree.

"It's against the law to mes, to mes—I mean to mesmerize," said Jack, staring severely at the strange apparition. "Ozma has forbidden the practise of magic in Oz. Don't you know that?"

"I know no law but the law of Belfaygor of Bourne," said the old man haughtily.

"And who is Belfaygor," inquired Peter, standing up on the Iffin's back to get a better view of this curious person.

"Lord of these Lands, and my illustrious Master. Alas! Alas! What have I done! Unhappy him! Unhappy I! Unhappy us. I am a mess! I am a mess! A most mis-er-able mesmerizer." Burying his face in his hands, the old man rushed blindly past them, and long after he had gone his piercing groans came echoing back to them.

"Now what do you suppose he did do?" asked Peter, settling himself thoughtfully between the Iffin's wings.

"Belfaygor, Belfaygor," mused Snif, repeating the name over several times. "I remember now—he's one of the good barons. Let's go on to his castle and see what has happened to him." But they did not have to wait till they reached the castle to find out, for halfway through the park, they came upon the baron himself. His ruby crown, magnificent red boots, richly embroidered cape, proclaimed his rank at once, but it was his beard that Peter saw first and never forgot afterward—a red beard

64

that flashed and flowed down his breast and swirled around his feet in an angry red tide. With his head thrown back, a pair of shears in each hand, Belfaygor was clipping desperately at the shining waves that seemed to pour in a steady torrent from his chin. At each clip he groaned and at each groan he clipped.

"My beard!" choked the baron. "My bride and my beard!" My bride and my beard!" And so engrossed and distressed was the unhappy gentleman that he neither saw nor heard the Iffin's approach.

"So this is what comes of mesmerizing," snorted Snif, stopping so suddenly he almost unseated his riders. "His beard is running away with him. What can we do about it?"

"Can we be of any help?" called Peter, more practically. "Is there anything we can do Mr. Baron?" At Peter's question, Belfaygor gave a great start; then blinking up half-seeingly at the strange company, gloomily shook his head.

"Nothing can help me," moaned the baron, clipping furiously, "for nothing can stop this beard from growing. And that's not the worst, Mogodore the Mighty has stolen the Princess I was to marry and each time I try to run to rescue her my beard trips me up. Woe, woe, woe! Was ever a man so unhappy—so unlucky as I?"

"Where are your men," asked Snif, wrinkling up his nose anxiously.

"Gone," said the Baron dully. "Frightened

"MISERABLE MESMERIZER," REPEATED THE BARON DULLY.

off by my beard, they have deserted me down to the smallest train bearer."

"You don't need a train bearer. What you need is a beard bearer," puffed Jack Pumpkinhead, dismounting stiffly and stepped as close as he dared to the baron. "If you throw your beard over your shoulder, it will grow the other way," he suggested amiably. For a moment Belfaygor stared slowly at Jack, then flinging the red beard over one shoulder he extended both arms.

"That's the only sensible thing I've heard since I was mesmerized," he shouted hoarsely. "I hereby appoint you Royal Bearer of the beard."

"Thanks," murmured Jack, looking doubtfully at Peter.

"Who are you?" demanded the baron in growing excitement and appreciation. "This Griffin I have seen before, but you, my good fellow are most odd and curious.

"He is a Pumpkinhead, magically brought to life," volunteered Peter. "And some pumpkins," he finished, with a wink at the Iffin.

"No, only one," corrected Jack modestly. "I am a subject of Ozma of Oz and this boy is from America. As we are all on our way to the Emerald City, I cannot bear your beard."

"Neither can I," mourned the Baron, dropping his arms wearily. "Oh! Oh! Who will save poor little Shirley Sunshine?" The Baron looked so tired and dejected that Peter felt sorry for him.

"Is Shirley Sunshine the Princess you are to marry?" he asked curiously. "Who is this Mogodore? Why not tell us the whole story, maybe we can help you?"

"If wings will help and a magic sack,
You'll soon have your little Princess back,"

promised the Iffin, sitting on his haunches beside Peter. "Speak," he urged, raising his claw imperiously. "Speak, for we are all attention."

CHAPTER 7

Belfaygor's Strange Story

W ITH a gusty sigh, the red baron looked from one to another and then, fixing his eyes sadly on Peter, he began to speak. Since the extremely sensible suggestion of Jack Pumpkinhead, his beard no longer poured round his ankles but, sweeping over his shoulder, disappeared in a red streak between the trees. Every little while he would cut it off, and the steady snip-snip of the shears ran like a sharp punctuation all through the strange story of his misfortune.

"This morning," confided Belfaygor in a mournful voice, "this morning I was the happiest Lord in the Land, for my marriage with Shirley Sunshine, whose father lives on the next hillside, had been satisfactorily arranged. My palace had been redecorated to please the Princess and all my retainers newly outfitted for the wedding. Everything, in fact, was in readiness to receive her, and I myself was about to start for her father's castle, when I became suddenly dissatisfied with my appearance." Overcome by his feelings the baron paused for a full moment, and Peter stood up on Snif's back to see how far the red beard had grown since the last clip. With a little gasp he saw it shoot through the branches of a tall tulip tree, and as he sat down Belfaygor tearfully continued his recital.

"So I sent for my chief mesmerizer," he said sorrowfully, "a good old man and exceedingly well versed in necromancy. I asked him if it would be possible to grow a beard, as I felt that a fine long beard would greatly improve my appearance. There was not time to grow one naturally, so this mesmerizer——"

"This miserable mesmerizer," corrected the Iffin, switching his tail furiously.

"Miserable mesmerizer," repeated the baron dully, "caused a long red beard to grow upon my chin." Snipping off a silky length of the offending whiskers, he tossed the ends over one shoulder and with a deep sigh proceeded. "When the beard had grown to my waist I bade the mesmerizer stop it, but in spite of all his incantations and magic powders, it continued to grow. It grew and grew till it filled the throne room, ran down the stairs into the pantry, shot up the stairs into the bed rooms and finally filled every room in the palace. In real danger of suffocation, my knights and servants took to their heels, and my mesmerizer, after forcing these shears upon me and bidding me cut for dear life, ran off and left me, also."

"Then how did you get out of the castle," asked Peter, lurching forward, while Jack leaned over so far his head fell off and had to be replaced by the Iffin.

"Jumped out a window," explained the Baron with a little shudder. "The beard kept me from breaking any bones. Cutting myself loose from the terrible tangle, I ran into the middle of the road and called loudly for help. As I did, a commotion on the next hillside attracted my attention. A band of armed riders were galloping toward me. As they drew nearer, I recognized the plumed hats and golden spears of Mogodore's retainers, and as they came nearer still I saw that Mogodore himself was carrying off my bride, who lay unconscious across his saddle bow. I tried to scream, but the red beard enveloped me. I tried to run; it tripped me at every step. Without even seeing me, the

calvacade thundered by. As they disappeared, I heard two of the riders boasting that Mogodore would marry Shirley Sunshine tomorrow morning."

"When was that? Where did he take her?" gasped Peter. "How long ago was it?"

"This morning," choked Belfaygor. "He has carried her to his castle in Baffleburg."

"You mean to say all of your men ran off and never came back?" exclaimed Peter, springing up indignantly. "Well, don't you care. We're here now and I'm sure Ozma would want us to help you. We'll just fly on Snif's back to Baffleburg and snatch her away from this bandit."

"I'm afraid you have never heard of Mogodore," interrupted the baron, shaking his head despairingly. "No one has ever entered the City of Baffleburg or returned alive from Mogodore's mountain."

"If that is so, we'll be the first;
To tame this wretch or know the worst,"

roared the Iffin, coming to his feet with a bound.

"I guess you never heard of Peter," said Jack Pumpkinhead, rising with great dignity. "This boy"—he waved impressively in Peter's direction—"has just conquered the entire City of Scares and the last time he was in Oz he saved the Emerald City from the Gnome King."

While Belfaygor looked incredulously at the little boy, Jack told of their morning's experiences in Chimneyville and Scare City.

"Have you still got the pirate's sack?" asked Belfaygor, forgetting to clip his beard in his extreme interest and astonishment. "That magic dinner bell—what is it? Do you suppose you could carry us all to Baffleburg?" Eagerly he turned to Snif. The Iffin raised both of his powerful wings and shook his head confidently, while Jack held up the dinner bell and Peter showed the famous sack.

"We'll be there in no time," cried Peter, "and with all this magic I don't see how Mogodore can conquer us, do you?"

Belfaygor was so cheered and encouraged by this little speech that he dropped both pairs of shears and embraced Peter upon the spot.

"You shall be knighted for this, my boy," he promised. "You, too," he added, pressing Jack's wooden fingers earnestly.

"What about me?" inquired Snif, raising a claw solemnly.

"If this keeps up we'll all be knighted;
Sir Jack! Sir Pete, why am I slighted?"

"You're not," promised Belfaygor, quickly picking up his shears and beginning to snip furiously. "You'll be knighted, too."

"Well, if you insist," murmured the Iffin in a mollified tone, "but I won't wear armor.

Come on knights," he called gaily, "for night is coming on and if we're to reach Baffleburg before dark we'd better start now."

The very name of Baffleburg gave Peter a thrill. More interested and excited than he had been since his arrival in Oz, he helped Jack to mount the Iffin's back and hurriedly seated himself behind him. Belfaygor came next with his back to Peter, so his beard would not blow in the little boy's face, and after a glance back to see that his riders were safe and comfortable, Snif spread his great wings and soared aloft, flying straight toward the red mountains Peter had seen in the distance. As they rose higher and higher Belfaygor found it no longer necessary to ply his shears, and his bright red beard streamed like a waving banner behind them. The poor baron was glad indeed for this rest, for he had been clipping steadily since early morning and already had blisters on both thumbs. Now and then, when his beard seemed in danger of catching in a tree or winding about a castle tower, he would snip it off short again and Peter and Jack would watch it float away, like some strange red cloud.

Flying was such an exhilarating experience that Peter forgot all about the dangerous adventure that lay ahead and the forbidding aspect of Mogodore's mountain did not trouble him at all. As they drew closer, he could see the City of Baffleburg, its turreted forts, and its castle and strong houses seeming to spring

from the rock itself. Stretching round the mountain there was a yawning chasm and at the foot was a towered fortress and drawbridge over which Mogodore and his men crossed the chasm when they made war on the barons below. Red capped warriors stood in each embrasure of the fort and guards marched stiffly to and fro upon the city walls. The grim red castle clung to the rocks, halfway up the mountain and gave Mogodore a splendid view of the whole valley beneath.

"If I fly too near, a golden spear may interrupt our flight;
So let's descend and mix a little stratagem with might."

muttered the Iffin, coasting cautiously downward.

"Stratagem's a big word," sighed Jack Pumpkinhead. "What does it mean?"

"A plan to confuse the enemy," explained Peter as the Iffin's feet touched the rocky ground on the other side of the chasm. "We must find the best place to drop into the city, the best way to use the pirate's sack and the quickest plan for finding the Princess."

Belfaygor was the first to dismount. Throwing his beard impatiently over his shoulder, he frowned gloomily up at the Mogodore's mountain. Now that they were really before the City of Baffleburg, the cheerful plans and hopes of Peter and the Iffin seemed wild and impractical.

The longer he looked the more impossible they seemed, and resting his hand heavily on Peter's shoulder he begged the little boy to continue his journey to the Emerald City and leave him to deal with the wicked mountain chief.

"The Iffin can carry me into the city," sighed Belfaygor, "but I cannot let you share in the awful perils of this undertaking." If Peter had not been in Oz, or addressing a baron, he might have answered, "Applesauce." But feeling that such a word would only puzzle this dignified nobleman, he seated himself on the nearest rock and looked curiously across the chasm.

"I should think," mused Peter, "that the best plan would be to fly into the city under cover of darkness and drop into the castle courtyard. Once inside, I will open the pirate's sack and when it has swallowed Mogodore and all the fighting men we can safely search for the Princess and escape."

"How do you know the sack won't swallow her too?" questioned Belfaygor uneasily.

"Because," said Peter looking up at the tallest tower in the castle, "I believe she's locked up there. They always lock the Princess up in the tower," he finished confidently.

"You think of everything." Jack Pumpkinhead stared down at the little boy admiringly and Snif, who had been scouting around for a stray geranium, waved an approving claw at Peter.

"If that's the plan, let's have a bite;
And quietly stay here till night!"

"But what shall we eat?" said Belfaygor, clipping at his whiskers despondently. Jack chuckled at this, and drawing out the Red Jinn's bell rang it imperiously. At once the little black slave, bearing his silver tray, appeared before them. Placing the tray on Peter's knees he faded out of sight so suddenly that Belfaygor dropped his shears with a clatter. Though he had heard about the magic dinner bell the unexpected appearance of the dinner quite upset him.

"You take this one," said Peter generously, "and if you sit with your back to the chasm and throw your beard over your shoulder it will grow down into the opening and let you eat in peace."

"How can I ever thank you?" exclaimed the baron, seating himself as the little boy suggested. "Odds pasties, this looks most tempting!" With a long, tremulous sigh, Belfaygor fell upon the appetizing repast of roast beef and plum pudding. Then Jack rang the bell again and the slave appeared with a tray for Peter. He was about to ring up another dinner for Snif but the Iffin shook his head.

"I've had enough for one day," he told them firmly, "and if Peter will give me that bunch of violets, everything will be perfectly perk!" As an extra touch a small bunch of violets had been placed beside Peter's dinner plate. Tossing them gaily to the Iffin and thinking as he did so how curious it was here for so huge a beast to dine upon flowers, Peter started in on his own dinner. With both hands clasped behind him, Jack watched the sun sink down behind the grim red mountain, and Peter and Belfaygor were so hungry that neither spoke till all the plates on their trays were empty. Then, with a satisfied sigh, Peter stood up and as the trays disappeared began looking around for Snif. But there was no sign of the Iffin anywhere!

"Oh!" gasped Peter anxiously, forgetting for the moment that Snif could fly, "he must have fallen into the chasm." Calling to Jack and the baron, he started to run along the edge of the ravine, striking impatiently at a small creature that kept beating its wings in his face. He thought he had brushed it aside when, with an angry screech, it fastened its claws in his shoulder.

> "If you hit me again, I'll bite your ear;
> Attention! Pause! Stop! Look and hear!"

At the familiar verses, Peter did stop, and glancing down he saw a creature no bigger than a squirrel perched on his shoulder.

"It's me," wailed a desperate voice, as the tiny beast leaned over and rubbed its head against his cheek.

"Those violets," it choked bitterly, "those violets were shrinking violets, Peter. Look at me! I've shrunk! I might just as well throw myself away."

"Don't," gulped Peter, as the Iffin started to hurl itself from his shoulder. "I like you little."

"Well I like him big," announced Jack unfeelingly. "And who's to carry us over the chasm now, may I ask?"

"Oh!" groaned Belfaygor, tripping over his whiskers after one horrified look at the little monster, "everything is over! Everything is over now!"

"So's your old beard," mumbled Jack in an annoyed voice. Picking up the shears Belfaygor had dropped he cut length after length from the enchanted red beard, while the baron continued to wring his hands and groan and Peter tried in vain to comfort the Iffin.

CHAPTER 8

A Way to Cross the Chasm

"I'LL WAGER that old Jinn did this on purpose," declared Jack indignantly. "I'll ring that dumbbell again and the boy's neck, too!"

"It wasn't his fault," put in Peter, lifting Snif from his shoulder and thoughtfully stroking the small red head. "I don't suppose those violets were meant to be eaten."

"If I only hadn't eaten them," wailed the

A Way to Cross the Chasm

Iffin, as two tears rolled down his cheeks. "You've no idea how it feels to shrink, boys.

> "Why did I eat those violets. I feel so sil and small!
> I'm just an elf, I'm not myself, I'm just no one at all!"

"Oh, yes you are," Peter reassured him hastily. "Why look, you'll fit right in my pocket and I'll carry you for a change and when we reach the Emerald City the Wizard of Oz will soon make you large again."

"Are we to reach the Emerald City?" inquired Jack, looking up from snipping Belfaygor's beard. "And how do you know you won't shrink yourself?"

Peter turned a little pale at Jack's question.

"The baron and I didn't eat any violets," he answered, swallowing hastily.

"Yes, but how are we to cross the chasm?" Belfaygor, taking the shears from Jack, rolled his eyes sadly at Peter.

"We'll just have to think of some other way," said Peter, staring off at Mogodore's mountain. "Let's all think."

"I can only think of poor little Shirley Sunshine, locked up in that dismal tower," retorted Belfaygor despondently.

"I can only think how far it must be to the bottom of this crevice," muttered Jack, looking sadly down into the ravine.

"It looks to me as if we'd have to do all the thinking for this party," murmured Snif, flying up on Peter's shoulder. "Never mind, I still can think, even if I am little.

> "If I do a little thinking and I think a little bit,
> If there's any way to cross it, why I'll surely think of it!"

"I'm glad you can still make verses," said Peter with a sigh. "It helps, and makes things seem a little less awful."

"Yes," said the Iffin, resting his cheek against Peter's. The sun had dropped down behind the red castle and in the gray light of early evening the grim city on the rocks looked more forbidding than ever. Great black crows circled about the towers and turrets and their hoarse crys drifted like threatening jeers across the chasm.

"If we had an ax," said Peter gloomily, "we might chop down a tree on the edge of the chasm so it would fall across." He was just wondering whether the ravine was narrow enough to jump at any point, when Snif gave a little bounce and, flying off his shoulder, announced shrilly: "I have thought of a way! We'll cross on the baron's beard!"

"You mean grow across?" asked Jack Pumpkinhead doubtfully.

"Impossible!" roared Belfaygor, throwing up his shears and hands indignantly. "Wouldst jerk out my whiskers? Besides they grow down and not up."

"Pause!" Holding up one claw, the Iffin looked solemnly from one to the other. "First," explained Snif quietly, "Belfaygor must walk three times around a tree. That will make his beard fast and keep it from pulling. Then I will take the end of the beard in my claws, fly across the chasm and fasten it to a tree on the other side. Then when Peter and Jack have crossed, the Baron can snip off the beard close to his chin and cross himself in safety. What think you of that, my brave comrades?"

"Why, that's a perfectly splendid idea!" cried Peter, jumping up enthusiastically. "How ever did you think of it?"

"Well," Snif reminded him gaily, "for five years I did nothing but think—so thinking comes easy to me. How about it Baron, will you lend us your beard?"

"Yes," answered Belfaygor readily enough, now that he had heard the Iffin's plan, "even if it hurts I will do it. I'll do anything to save Shirley Sunshine from that villainous bandit."

"Then everything's settled!" cried Peter, who hated delay or inactivity of any kind. "Let's start!"

"Not now," said the Iffin, shaking his little head seriously. "We must wait till morning Peter. As I cannot carry you all up to the castle itself, you will have to climb over the rocks and cliffs to the city gates. This will be bad enough by daylight, but impossible at night."

"That's so," agreed Peter regretfully.

"And what's to become of us when we reach the city gates?" quavered Jack in a hollow voice. "Will not these Baffleburghers impale us upon their spears?"

"Oh, I hope not," muttered the Iffin, settling down on Peter's shoulder, "but we'll have to take a chance on it. My guess is that the guards will seize and carry you to Mogodore. Once in Mogodore's presence, Peter can open the sack, and after the sack swallows everyone, we'll find the Princess and return to the capitol on foot."

"What about my beard?" asked Belfaygor nervously. "If they make us prisoners and take away my shears, we'll all be smothered."

"Well, so will they," Snif reminded him philosophically, "and that will be some comfort." Already Snif seemed to have forgotten his dreadful mishap and to have recovered his former good spirits, and under the influence of the merry little monster the whole party grew quite cheerful and gay.

"Come along," he called, flying on ahead, "Let's find some place to sleep. Is that a cave I see over there?"

Back among the rocks at the foot of a tall cliff there was a cave, sure enough, and Peter, after a little exploring, decided it would be just the place in which to spend the night. Lengths cut from Belfaygor's beard and piled on the floor made splendid mattresses and, as Jack Pumpkinhead required no rest, he offered to stand guard at the entrance. The baron himself lay with his head just outside the cave, and the obliging Pumpkinhead promised to cut his beard from time to time and see that it did not choke up the opening, nor suffocate the sleepers. So much had happened since Peter fell into the pumpkin field, he was weary as a walrus and glad enough to rest. By the time the moon had climbed to the top of Mogodore's mountain, he was fast asleep, the Iffin curled cozily in the bend of his arm, and soon only the snores of Belfaygor and the snip of Jack's shears broke the deep dark silence of the night.

CHAPTER 9

The Forbidden
Flagon

WHILE Peter and his friends rested in
their hidden cave, the lights in the
castle across the chasm burned far into the
night, as the Baron of Baffleburg sat in converse
with Wagarag, his chief steward and Major
Domo. Biggen and Little, the baron's body
guards, dozed stiffly at their posts behind his
chair, while the huge hunting dogs snored upon
the hearthstones. Flaring torches, set in stone
holders in the wall, flung a flickering light into
the dim corners of the great stone hall. Bear

rugs were strewn about the flagged floor; swords, daggers and glittering armor hung upon the walls and the furniture, the carved chests, tables and chairs were big and clumsy, like the owner of the castle himself.

With his chin resting in the palm of his hand, Mogodore stared moodily into the fire, but Wagarag, a thin anxious little Baffleburgher, moved about restlessly, straightening a tapestry here, a table cover there, and never still for a moment.

"If I only I knew what was in that miserable flagon," muttered the baron for about the fiftieth time. "If I only knew! Why must it be hidden? Why is it forbidden? What would happen if I broke the seal?"

"Buttered billygoats," spluttered Wagarag impatiently. "On the very eve of your wedding must you still worry about that wretched flask? Can you think of nothing but that miserable flagon?"

Flicking at a bit of gold dust on the mantel, Wagarag paused in exasperation before his master.

"If your father and grandfather before you were able to guard and keep it safely why cannot you let it rest where no one will discover its secret? Is it not written in the Book of Baffleburg that if aught disturbs the seal on the forbidden flagon, or one drop of the contents spills, a dreadful disaster will befall? Are you not Mogodore the Mighty, slayer of an hundred

bears, subduer of an hundred barons and Lord
of this mountain? Have you not stolen for your
bride the loveliest Princess in the valley? Pray
dismiss this mischievous flagon from your mind.
Think of something else," begged Wagarag
earnestly.

"Something pleasant, this Princess for in-
stance."

Wagarag clasped his hands and rolled his
eyes upward. "A beauteous damsel, if I may be
permitted to say so!"

"But she refuses to marry me," growled
Mogodore, crossing his legs irritably.

"What difference does that make," sniffed
Wagarag, poking the fire energetically. "Your
word is law in Baffleburg. Marry her anyway!"

"But I can't understand it," breathed Mogodore, taking up a mirror that lay on the arm of
his chair and surveying himself long and
earnestly. The reflection in the mirror stared
as earnestly back, but Mogodore could see
nothing amiss with the red face, bristling black
whiskers and hair, small blue eyes, great nose
and crooked mouth that confronted him. "No,
it cannot be my looks," grunted the baron,
setting down the mirror. "What does this
precious Princess want?" he demanded fret-
fully.

"Why not ask her?" suggested Wagarag,
prodding Biggen and Little vigorously in the
ribs. "Here, you lazy rogues, fetch down the
Princess from the tower!"

"Mayhap the Princess sleepeth," mumbled Biggen, rubbing his eyes and yawning terrifically.

"Then wakeneth her and bringeneth her thither," commanded Wagarag, giving Biggen a push and Little a poke.

But the Princess, as you may well imagine, was far from sleeping. Pacing restlessly up and down the small tower room, she was trying to think of some way to escape, and when Biggen and Little thumped on the door and explained that her presence was desired below, she went readily enough, hoping it might give her another chance to plead with the baron for her liberty, or wheedle the guards into releasing her. But Biggen and Little paid small attention to her entreaties. Roughly thrusting back the ruby necklace she offered if they would help her slip out of the castle, they picked her up bodily and carried her down to their master.

"Well!" exclaimed Mogodore, as Shirley Sunshine drew herself up proudly against one of the great stone pillars, "do you still refuse to marry me."

"Of course," answered the little Princess haughtily. "Release me at once or my father and Belfaygor will come and destroy you utterly."

"Destroy me!" roared the Baron, with an evil wink at Wagarag. "Do you not know that I am Mogodore the Mighty, boldest of all the barons and Lord of this mountain?"

"Only one mountain," said the Princess shaking back her long brown curls scornfully. "If you are as mighty as you pretend, I should think you'd conquer several."

"There are no more mountains worth conquering," stormed Mogodore, thumping the arm of his chair with his fist, "and you know that well enough."

"Yes, but there are other countries," said the Princess haughtily. Seeing the baron give a surprised start, and realizing that he was as vain as he was cruel, Shirley decided to flatter her villainous conqueror and delay the wedding by any trick or plan she could manage. "If I had your strength and fighting ability, I'd conquer and keep on conquering until I was a King," said the Princess, with an imperious gesture.

"Would you like me better if I were a King?" asked Mogodore, leaning forward eagerly. The Princess nodded so emphatically that her curls danced briskly to and fro and with a cry that shook the very rafters Mogodore leaped out of his chair.

"Then I'll be a King!" he shouted exuberantly. "I'll march across the Red Mountains, capture the Emerald City, depose this foolish little fairy Ozma and proclaim myself King of Oz."

"Better let well enough alone," cautioned Wagarag, running anxiously after his master, who was striding excitedly up and down the hearth. "There is a Wizard in the Emerald City who is exceedingly powerful and Ozma herself is a practiced magician."

"Puff on their magic," cried Mogodore, snapping his fingers contemptuously. "How can Ozma, who is small and weak, overcome a big fellow like me? Nay—argue not. I'll conquer the Emerald City and be a King, King Mogodore the First of Oz. I wonder I never thought of it myself. You're going to be a great help to me, my dear!"

Pausing before the Princess, Mogodore patted her clumsily on the head. "And what's more, you shall accompany me to the capitol, see this capturing done, be married in the Emerald City and crowned with Ozma's crown," he promised recklessly. "But now you must have some rest, for we'll start to-morrow morning.

"See that I'm called early," he blustered, shaking his finger at Wagarag. "See that my fighting men are roused at daybreak," he roared, knocking the heads of Biggen and Little smartly together. "When I'm King of Oz I can open that forbidden flagon," he confided hoarsely, leaning down to whisper in Wagarag's ear.

"No more of this wretched wondering. What will Baffleburg matter when I'm King of the realm? I'll put an end to this unbearable mystery. This Princess has brought me luck. Come kiss me, little one!"

But Shirley Sunshine, with a horrified glance at the boisterous Baron, picked up her skirts and fled from the room.

"See that she does not escape," rumbled Mogodore indulgently, and Biggen and Little, clattering after the Princess, locked her securely in the tower. Alone in the comfortless room, the captive Princess leaned against the barred windows and, fixing her eyes upon one steadfast star, wondered how long it would be before Belfaygor or her father came to rescue her. Her heart sank at the thought of this cruel baron marching upon the Emerald City, laying waste its parks and palaces and enslaving all of its gay and gentle inhabitants. Terrified by the frightful forces she had sets in motion, the tired little Princess threw herself upon the hard bed and cried herself to sleep.

Below in the castle hall, Wagarag endeavored to turn the baron from his audacious purpose. "Listen not to this mischievous maiden," begged the steward. "Stay here where you are known and powerful. It is better to be a ruler among fools than a fool among rulers. Many have

attempted to conquer the Kingdom of Oz—not one has succeeded."

"Then I will be the first," boasted Mogodore and, snatching a broad sword from the wall, he swung it expertly round his head. "Shine up your shin guards, Waggy old lad, for you're going with me and I hereby appoint you Royal Chancellor of Oz! Keeper of the King's Custard and Imperial Purveyor of Puddings!"

Laughing uproariously, Mogodore brought the flat of his sword down with a resounding thwack upon the thin shoulders of his disapproving steward.

"Come to bed, Dunce!" he cried good naturedly. "You mean well, but know nothing."

"At least I know my place," muttered Wagarag, shaking his head gloomily. "We both belong on this mountain and no good will come of this expedition."

"You forget the flagon," exulted Mogodore. "I shall at last know the secret of the forbidden flagon."

"Have it your own way," sighed Wagarag, with a resigned shrug. "But don't blame me if we're all turned to sticks by the Wizard of Oz and thrown into the fire."

"Ha! Ha!" shouted Mogodore, more amused than frightened by this terrible threat. "You'll make a splendid stick, old fellow." Laughing noisely, the bad, bold baron tramped cheerfully off to bed.

CHAPTER 10

The City of Baffleburg

A STRANGE, shrill squeaking wakened
Peter next morning, and starting up he
saw that it was the Iffin. Sitting on a flat stone,
the tiny monster was practising his gr-rrs. "If
I could only growl again, I wouldn't mind my
size," mourned Snif, looking sadly up at Peter.
"Can't fight! Can't growl! A fine fix for a
fabulous monster!"

"But you can think," answered Peter cheerfully. "And you're free. Just wait till we've

conquered this silly old baron and come to the Emerald City. You'll be a sure-enough griffin then. But I kinda like you little," he added loyally, "and I should think it would be rather an interesting experience."

"Well," acknowledged the Iffin, scratching his ear reflectively with his third hind claw, "at least it will be something to tell my grandchildren, if I ever have any grandchildren." Raising his voice to a tiny roar he rushed to the front of the cave calling loudly, "What ho without!"

"I do not see a hoe of any kind," answered Jack Pumpkinhead blandly. "But the sun is up and the wind is changing and unless we move away from here we'll be buried in whiskers."

Stepping outside Peter saw a red mound as huge as ten hay stacks rolled into one. All night Jack had faithfully cut Belfaygor's beard and raked the cut lengths neatly together, but now the wind was whirling the top off the stack and filling the air with a blinding tangle of red strands. Hastily waking the Baron, the four adventurers hurried to the other side of the cliff and watched the great red cloud sweep into the chasm.

"And now to beard this baron in his den," proposed Snif, swinging himself gaily back and forward on the branches of a small tree.

"Yes, let us be off at once," sighed Belfaygor, taking the shears from Jack and starting in on his weary work of clipping.

"Let's have breakfast," suggested Peter, who was always hungriest in the morning. "Ring the old bell Jack."

"Then good-bye," quavered Snif, flying into the air. "I'll be back when those trays have disappeared and not before. No more magic repasts for me!"

While Peter and Belfaygor breakfasted royally on beef steak and fried potatoes, Snif nibbled daintily at the red honeysuckle that clung to the rocks and muttered little iffish verses to himself.

"Have you ever been to Baffleburg," asked Peter, after the trays had vanished and Snif came back to perch upon his shoulder. "Is it so very dangerous?"

"I have flown over Mogodore's mountain many times," said Snif thoughtfully, "and from what I have seen, it must be pretty bad.

"But if we stick together and most bravely persevere,
This mountain's dangers we'll surmount and tweak yon bandit's ears!"

"No tweaking," advised Jack Pumpkinhead nervously. "Let us just sack the city and leave."

"All right," agreed Snif good naturedly, but we can't leave till we start, so let's get started." He looked inquiringly at Belfaygor and Belfaygor, after a nervous glance across the chasm, stepped to a tree on the edge of the ravine and walked solemnly three times round, till his beard was securely fastened. Now that the time for action had come, the adventurers said little. Belfaygor stood proudly erect, waiting for his beard to grow long enough to stretch across the chasm and soon it did, and Snif, taking the ends in his claws, flew over the deep ravine and fastened the beard tightly to a tree on the other side. Now, all was ready and Peter, dropping boldly over the edge, swung himself skillfully across on the swinging red cable. He dared not look down and once safely over watched uneasily while Jack pulled himself across.

"Whatever you do, don't lose your head," breathed Peter, leaning forward nervously. Halfway over, Jack's wooden fingers almost lost their hold, and his pumpkin head spun about upon its peg, but Snif, flying valiantly to the rescue, held it in place and, when at last Jack came near enough for Peter to reach, he clutched both wooden arms and dragged Jack thankfully to safety. Belfaygor now clipped off his beard close to the chin and crossed himself without mishap or difficulty.

The first step of the dangerous undertaking had been made in safety but straight ahead was a steep wall of rock. If it had not been for Belfaygor's beard they would never have been able to scale this dreadful precipice. But Snif, taking the beard in his claws, flew up till he found a boulder or sturdy sapling. Then, winding the beard several times round, he would signal to Belfaygor who would immediately snip off his end of the beard and climb expertly up the swinging rope. Peter, hoisting himself up after him, could not help but think what a splendid Alpine guide the baron would make. But Jack, tremblingly following Peter, resolved that if ever he reached the Emerald City again he would stay peaceably at home for the rest of his unnatural life.

In this interesting but perilous fashion they finally reached the top of the cliff, only to find the gates of the city still farther up. A rocky opening into a narrow tunnel apparently led directly to Baffleburg and, with many misgivings, the travellers entered the tunnel. Although it was dark and clammy inside and exceedingly rough underfoot, they reached the end without trouble. In the dim murky light Peter saw a wooden door with an iron ring in the center. He was about to grasp the ring, when the tunnel, without any warning, tipped downward and shot them headlong from the opening. Snatching at a tree just in time, Peter saved himself from pitching over the precipice. Belfaygor's beard, catching on a jagged rock saved him and fortunately the baron had hold of Jack. His head did bounce off, but by some miracle rolled into a hollow in the rocks. Snif went over the edge of the cliff, but spreading his wings flew back to safety.

"Something else to tell my grandchildren,"

grumbled the Iffin, shaking himself angrily, while Peter hastily recovered Jack's pumpkin head and put it back where it belonged. "I'll pay him up for that slide. Come on boys, let's try it again. Can a trick tunnel hold us back now?"

Peter looked inquiringly at Belfaygor and Belfaygor clipping a length from his beard looked doubtfully at Peter but Jack, holding his head with both hands, expressed in no uncertain terms his complete unwillingness to ever enter the treacherous tunnel again.

"But we must go on," said Snif stubbornly:

> "If we will just consider, we'll find some simple way
> To tread this tipsy tunnel, and we'll try it, come what may!"

"Well I'm not May, and I think the way we came was simple enough," complained Jack. "I never felt more simple in my life, and look at the dent in my head!"

"Maybe if we run through as fast as we can and get hold of the iron ring in the door before the tunnel tilts we won't spill out," suggested Peter, examining a long scratch on his knee. "I'll go first," he volunteered gamely, "and all of you can hold on to me." Snif and Belfaygor immediately approved of this plan and Jack finally, not desiring to be left, consented to go. First Peter put Snif in his pocket, then Belfaygor

105

BELFAGOR CLIPPED OFF HIS BEARD AND CROSSED, HIMSELF, WITH-
OUT MISHAP OR DIFFICULTY.

caught hold of Peter's coat tails and Jack caught hold of Belfaygor's. Taking a long breath, Peter dashed into the tunnel and never, even when he was making a home run, had he sprinted along any faster, Jack and the Baron clattering along as best they could behind him.

Just as Peter reached the tunnel end and grasped the iron ring, the tunnel tipped a second time. But Peter hung on to the ring and others hung on to Peter. Several coat seams ripped, but when the tunnel finally righted itself they were still inside. Before it could tilt again, Peter turned the ring, opened the wooden door and stepped into a large cobble-stone courtyard.

Straight ahead rose the grim gray walls and buttressed towers of Baffleburg. As they tiptoed nearer, they could hear the sharp ring of horses' hoofs on the other side of the wall.

"Shall I fly over and see what's going on?" asked Snif, fluttering excitedly out of Peter's pocket.

"No! No!" begged the little boy hurriedly. "Let's all stay together. I'll ring that bell over the city gates and when the guards carry us to Mogodore we'll open the sack as we planned!" Running forward, Peter seized the chain attached to a huge bell over the gates and gave it a tremendous pull. It was impossible to see into Baffleburg, as the gates were backed with panels of wood and the walls themselves were high as sky scrapers. As the wild clanging of the bell died away, the four adventurers drew closer together. But nothing at all happened. Again Peter jerked the iron chain but still no one came to open the gates.

"They refuse to admit us," puffed Belfagor, with a furious clip at his whiskers. "What now?" Before they had time to decide upon any plan, four towers rising from the city's walls suddenly tilted downward, and shooting from their tops came a perfect shower of golden spears. Throwing themselves flat upon the cobbles, Peter and his companions managed to escape injury. Time and again the tilting towers rose and fell, spraying the courtyard with spears. By crawling close to the walls and lying perfectly flat, the four adventurers were able to keep out of their way, but as Peter reflected gloomily, they could not lie under the wall forever. He was considering whether or not to open the pirate's sack and see if it would swallow the spears, when Belfaygor touched him on the shoulder.

"When the tower nearest me tilts again, I shall jump in the window," whispered the baron. "You and Jack must follow. By keeping directly under the tower you will avoid the spears.

"Wait!" gasped Peter, horrified at Belfaygor's daring scheme. But Belfaygor, shaking his head determinedly, leaped to his feet, and as the tower came tilting down he plunged headfirst into the window nearest to the ground.

"Hooka-ma-roosters!" choked the Iffin. "How did he do that?"

"How are we to do it?" panted Peter, as all four towers shot up into place again. Motionless and terrified they waited for them to descend, but the Baffleburghers, evidently deciding that their visitors were utterly routed, had turned off the machinery and all four towers stopped tilting. There was no possible way into the city now, and completely baffled Peter stared angrily up at the thick gray walls.

"Now I'll have to fly over," muttered Snif nervously. "Maybe I can open the gates."

"A signal!" called Jack suddenly. "A signal! Squash and turnip tops! It's Belfaygor's beard!" Looking where Jack pointed, Peter and the Iffin saw Belfaygor himself outlined in the window of the nearest tower. And pouring over the sill and growing steadily downward were the wonderful and ever dependable red whiskers.

"We can climb his beard," cried Peter excitedly. "Come on, it's almost long enough!"

This was evidently what Belfaygor intended, for when they looked again, they could see him twining his beard round a huge spike on the sill. Then he waved his hand, and Peter, tightening his belt, climbed boldly aloft, looking back now and then to call encouragement to Jack Pumpkinhead. In less than a minute they were all safely inside the tower, for the Iffin had flown up with no trouble at all. The tower room was cheerless and without furniture. A spiral stairway in the center led downward. At the thought of conquering another city, Peter's impatience and excitement grew. If only some of the boys could be along, or his grandfather! He tried to picture Belfaygor's amazement when the pirate's sack should come into action, and seizing the baron's arm fairly dragged him to the stair.

"I suppose if we go down these steps we'll come out in the courtyard, for this certainly is the fort," puffed Peter, clattering ahead.

"All we do is climb up and down," groaned Jack Pumpkinhead. "I'll bet it's a million steps to the bottom."

"Oh, not that many," grinned Peter, looking down at Snif, who was comfortably seated on his shoulder. Quietly cutting his beard Belfaygor stepped after Peter and Jack resignedly brought up at the end of the procession.

CHAPTER 11

In the Castle of Mogodore

"NOW TO get ourselves captured," whispered Peter eagerly, as they finally reached the bottom of the stair.

"It should not be difficult," answered Snif, who had flown ahead and now came back to rest on Peter's shoulder. "Behold! Be bold! Look! Gaze and tremble!" Stepping out of the dim tower into the courtyard of the fort, Peter gave a little whistle of consternation and surprise. Drawn up in glittering rows were a

113

thousand mounted men in armor, each holding a golden spear.

"Something's afoot here," muttered Belfaygor behind his waving whiskers.

"You mean a horse, don't you?" corrected Jack, straightening his head and dusting a cobweb off his chin. "Is that sack quite ready Peter?" Peter nodded and as one of the armored riders caught sight of the intruders and galloped furiously forward, he called boldly, "Conduct us to your chief. We have important tidings to impart."

"Impart them to me," ordered the horseman, lifting his visor and frowning down at the little boy. "Impart them to me, or I'll prick ye over yon wall."

> "If you so much as raise your spear. I'll bite
>   your nose, I'll chew your ear!
> You'll vanish, melt and disappear. We're all
>   magicians, do you hear?"

shrieked the Iffin, flying in dizzy circles about the rider's head.

"Avaunt varlet," rasped Belfaygor, tossing his beard over his shoulder with a lordly gesture, "our business is with your Master!" The circling little Iffin, the strange appearance of Jack Pumpkinhead and the wildly waving whiskers of Belfaygor all tended to bewilder the horseman. For a moment he hesitated, then galloping back, conferred anxiously with one of

his companions. After much head shaking and arm waving, they both rode forward, and beckoning for the travellers to follow them, trotted briskly under a stone archway that led up to the town itself.

"That was easy," chuckled Peter, trudging gaily after the mailed riders. "They think we're magicians, Snif."

"We'll have to be to get out of here," muttered the little monster uneasily. "Be careful, boy, be carefuller than careful!"

"Every step brings us nearer to the Princess," said Belfaygor, tripping over his beard and fixing his eyes hopefully on the castle tower. But it was many weary steps to the palace, and the one cobbled street of Baffleburg was both steep and narrow. Red stone cottages perched on the cliffs at either side, and now and then a curious head was stuck out as the little procession went pounding by. But at last they came to the red gates of the castle itself, and after a short parley with the guards were admitted. Leaving their horses in the courtyard, the two warriors hustled their charges into the baronial hall of the mountain chief. Looking around the great hall, Peter decided that it was just the kind of castle he had always dreamed of owning. His eyes shone as they rested on the jewelled swords and armor that decorated the walls. But he was quickly brought back to the dangerous business in hand by the stern voice of their guide.

"Magicians with an important message to impart," announced the first man, dipping his spear in a salute to Mogodore. In full fighting regalia, the Baron of Baffleburg sat at a long table in the center of the hall, poring over an old map of Oz and trying to decide at what point to attack the capitol. Back of him stood Wagarag, in a hastily assembled armor of iron pots and sauce pans. Next to Wagarag lounged Bragga, Captain of the Guard and Smerker, Chief Scorner of the realm.

"Magicians!" rumbled Mogodore looking up impatiently. "That accounts for them getting into the city. Magicians, eh! Well they look like a pack of peddlars. Scorn them," he ordered, contemptuously jerking his thumb at Smerker. Now Peter had never been scorned in his life and wanted to see how it was done. So instead of immediately opening the pirate's sack he stood staring curiously at Smerker. Leaning forward, the Chief Scorner seized a key-like handle that seemed to be attached to his nose and turned it straight upward. At the same time he curled back his lips in a truly astonishing manner.

"Ho! Ha! Ha!" roared Snif, holding on to Peter with both claws:

> "If this be scorning, we are scorned!
> With what a nose he is adorned."

Peter felt like laughing himself, but the Chief Scorner, paying no attention at all to the

Iffin, now snatched a sauce box from his sleeve and opening it with a quick jerk, held it out toward the travellers. Immediately the sauce box began to scold and berate them in the most harsh and abusive terms making more noise than a dozen radios and filling the air with such a horrid racket that Peter covered his ears and the others, without meaning to, backed toward the door. Satisfied that his Chief Scorner had subdued the intruders, Mogodore motioned for Smerker to close the sauce box.

"Now throw them out," he barked with a wave at Bragga. "I've wasted too much time already." But as Bragga stepped forward to obey this command, Belfaygor, snipping a long piece from his beard stepped boldly up to the baron and thumping his fist on the table demanded in a loud voice, "What have you done with my Princess? Where is Shirley Sunshine?"

Boldened by this spirited action, Jack Pumpkinhead stepped up beside him. "Release this maiden at once, you rude, rash robber, you— you Princess snapper," he cried.

"Have the sack ready, quick," whispered Snif to Peter, as Mogodore stared angrily at the strange pair.

"So that's it," grunted the Baron of Baffle-burg. "I see now that you are Belfaygor of Bourne, hiding like a coward behind false whiskers. Well, you shall not marry this Princess, for she is to marry me—Mogodore the Mighty!"

"Mighty what?" inquired Jack Pumpkinhead curiously.

"Mighty mighty, you impertinent fool, mighty important you ridiculous pumpkin head. Smite him," bellowed the Baron with a wrathful wave at Jack. "Remove this whiskered pest," he roared in the next breath with another wave at Belfaygor.

"So you're Mogodore the smite-y. Well don't you dare smite me," challenged Jack, shaking his wooden fist under Mogodore's nose. "There stands Peter, the pitcher from Philadelphia. On his shoulder sits a fabulous monster who may devour you any minute."

As Mogodore, rather startled by this long rigamarole, half rose in his chair, Jack vigorously rang the Red Jinn's bell and down upon the table flashed the little black slave, set down his tray and vanished. Mogodore's retainers screamed with fright, and the Baron himself blinked with astonishment, but when Jack rang the bell a second time, Biggen and Little sprang forward and seized the little slave by the wrists. In a twinkling the slave disappeared. Biggen and Little also disappeared.

"You see," quavered Jack in a slightly unsteady voice, "I am a great magician!"

"Then bring back my guards," yelled Mogodore, stamping his foot furiously.

"Give back my Princess," retorted Belfaygor just as furiously. Thinking it about time to put an end to this dangerous discussion, Peter pulled the pirate's sack from his shoulders and was about to unfasten the cord, when he was seized suddenly from behind and both arms pinioned closely to his sides.

"This pitcher's trying some more magic tricks," panted the spearman indignantly. He had crept up quietly behind Peter, and in spite of the little boy's struggles, Mogodore's big soldier held him fast.

"We hang pitchers on the wall here!" boomed Mogodore, glaring fiercely at Peter. (I regret to say the big baron did not know the difference between picture and pitcher.) "Hold that pitcher—seize that whiskered rascal and behead that pumpkinheaded dunce! Enough of this nonsense. When I return from the Emerald City I'll make them produce Biggen and Little and behead them all!" promised Mogodore, striding up and down with a great clash and clatter of armor. "Is Princess Shirley ready? I wait for no man and precious few women!"

"I will see, your Highness!" Touching the iron pot he was wearing for a helmet, Wagarag hurried from the hall and while Peter in helpless rage looked on, Bragga seized Belfaygor, the other spearman caught Jack and flung him across the center table and unfeelingly struck off his head. Such was the force of blow, Jack's pumpkin bounced to the floor, rolled through a tapestry-curtained door and disappeared. At this dreadful turn of affairs, Peter gave a groan and Snif almost succeeded in growling, but being unable to open the pirate's sack they were completely at the mercy of Mogodore and his men.

"Lock them up on the North tower till my return, and know that I will return a King," boasted Mogodore, placing his hand proudly upon the hilt of his sword. "We march upon the Emerald City this very morning, I'll marry Shirley Sunshine in the capitol and be crowned King of Oz before night fall."

"What!" gasped Peter, scarcely believing his ears.

"You'll be sorry for this," bawled Belfaygor, slashing with his shears at the Captain of the Guard. Poor Jack said nothing, for without a head what could he say? Threatening and struggling, Peter and Belfaygor were dragged off to the dungeons in the North tower, Snif doing what he could to release them by biting and scratching the hands and faces of the guards, but he was too little to help much and both were securely locked up. In his struggle with the spearman, Peter had dropped the pirate sack, and exhausted and discouraged he sank down on the stone bench in his dark little dungeon. The window was high above his head and let in only a feeble ray of light and the stone cell so small he could touch both sides by extending his arms. Snif had come with him, but Belfaygor had been locked in a dungeon

higher up in the tower. Things certainly had not gone as planned—in fact they were in worse plight than anyone could have imagined.

"Isn't this doggone?" groaned Peter glumly. "Jack's lost his head, I've lost the sack and Belfaygor will probably smother in whiskers! If someone doesn't warn Ozma, the Emerald City will be taken in no time. There's only one Knight and one soldier in the palace and the soldier can't fight at all. If Ozma doesn't know Mogodore is coming, so that she and the Wizard can start up their magic, they'll all be captured and the whole city destroyed. I wonder whatever put the notion of conquering Oz in Mogodore's head? Darn! Doggone! I wish I could get out of here!" Doubling up his fists, Peter pounded on the dungeon door.

"Maybe I can squeeze through the bars and fly off to warn Ozma of this villain's coming," said the Iffin, but the bars were so close together that even Snif could not slip through and in great discouragement the two prisoners sat side by side on the hard stone bench. Presently ten shrill blasts from the bugles and the clatter of hoofs on the cobbles below told that Mogodore had really started for the Emerald City.

"Now I'll never have any grandchildren," choked the Iffin, a tear trickling off the end of his nose.

"And I'll never get back to Philadelphia, or

be an air mail pilot," sighed Peter, clasping his hands behind his head and starting gloomily at the wall.

And I am sure each of you would have felt gloomy, if you had been in Peter's plight.

CHAPTER 12

The Escape from Baffleburg

A S THE rattle of hoofs and sound of bugles died away, Peter, looking down at Snif noticed that his eyes were growing larger and larger.

"Stop!" breathed Peter, nervously edging away and brushing his hand across his forehead.

"Stop what?" grunted the Iffin crossly. "I'm not doing anything."

"But your eyes," screamed Peter, edging still further away, "and your ears! Why your ears

are as big as you are. Help! Help! Look out.
Are you going to explode?"

Before Snif could touch his ear with his claw
or wonder what Peter was yelling about, he
expanded like a balloon, filling the entire
dungeon and squeezing Peter flat against the
wall. The effect of the shrinking violets had
worn off at last, and with the Iffin rapidly
reaching his former size and strength, there
was no room in the box-like cell. To keep from
crushing Peter, he pressed against the bars of
the dungeon. The force with which he shot up
to his full and former size tore the door from
its hinges and bent out the bars like wax.
While Snif stood terrified and trembling with
surprise, Peter, with great presence of mind,
pressed past him, slipped through the bent bars
and unlocked the dungeon door.

"We're free," gasped the little boy, as Snif
tumbled head first from their cell. "We're free
and you're big and strong again. We can fly to
the Emerald City right away and save Ozma
and everybody."

"If—I—ever—get—my—breath, you mean,"
wheezed Snif, leaning against the wall and
puffing like a porpoise. "Wh—ew! Growing up
is almost as bad as shrinking down."

"Did it hurt," asked Peter, eyeing his friend
with lively curiosity.

"Well, not exactly," explained the Iffin,
raising first one foot and then the other, "but

I've had lots more pleasant experiences. Did I hurt you?"

"Not much," said Peter, feeling a bruise on his elbow where he had been pressed against the wall. "Say, it's great to have you a monster again. Don't ever eat another violet as long as you live."

"I never will," shuddered the Iffin, shaking his head solemnly. "Out of my way, lump!" Pushing over a startled jailer who had run out to see what was the matter, Snif rushed along the corridor.

"First we'll find Belfaygor, then we'll hunt Jack's head and the pirate's sack and next we'll fly to the capitol and put an end to Mogodore's mischief. I can outfly a thousand horses without even trying," boasted Snif, pushing over another guard who darted out to intercept them.

"If I'd only opened that pirate's sack right away," puffed Peter running to catch up with Snif, "if I only had, all this would never have happened. Goodness, what's this?"

"Good news to me," chuckled Snif galloping along gaily. "It is Belfaygor's beard and will lead us straight to his dungeon." Snif was right. Trailing the flowing red whiskers of the baron, they came to the topmost cell in the tower. Out from the dungeon bars poured the enchanted beard of Belfaygor. Belfaygor, himself was leaning against the door, too discouraged and unhappy to even clip them once. But

when Peter called him by name, and he saw Snif grown to full size and power again, he snapped his shears joyfully and in a trembling voice demanded to know how they had come there.

"We burst our bars," cried Peter exuberantly. "At least Snif did." While the Iffin brushed the torrent of whiskers aside, the little boy unlocked the dungeon door, and after a hearty embrace told the baron all that had happened. Overjoyed at his release, Belfaygor followed them down the grim tower corridors. Each jailer who appeared was scornfully pushed aside by Snif, and when they came to the bottom Belfaygor and Peter seated themselves on his back and Snif rushed into the great stone hall of the castle. The few guards who had been left behind took to their heels as the Iffin flew screaming over their heads, and with no one to bother them the three began a systematic search for Jack's head. Jack's body was still sprawled over the center table. The top of his peg neck had been chopped off with his head, but whittling another point on the end, Peter gently dragged the headless figure to a chair and sat him down. Snif soon found the famous sack behind a screen, and remembering Jack's pumpkin had rolled through the door, Peter pushed aside the hanging and tiptoed into a long dim entry. It slanted slightly and Peter hurried along looking anxiously to the right and left, but the pumpkin head was nowhere to be seen. The hallway was growing narrower every minute, curving round and round like a spiral slideway and leading continuously downward. Peter was about to go back and call the others, when the moist nose of Snif appeared round one of the curves back of him.

"What's this?" demanded the Iffin. "And whither doth it lead?"

"I don't know," said Peter, "but Jack's head must have rolled down here and be lying somewhere at the bottom."

"Then let us join it by all means," chuckled the Iffin sitting down and sliding calmly after Peter. "Look out, here I come, and take this pirate's sack will you? It makes me positively shudder." Peter reached back and relieved Snif of the sack. Above they could hear Belfaygor treading cautiously down the hallway, but the curved passage soon grew so steep, Peter and Snif began to slip, roll and finally coast like children on a playground slide. "Now you've done it," coughed the Iffin as they finally

somersaulted into a dark cellarway, lit by one feeble lantern. "Out of one dungeon into another!"

"But there's Jack's head!" cried Peter, picking himself up joyfully. The sudden arrival of Belfaygor immediately knocked him down again, but while the baron mumbled apologies, Peter sprang to his feet, and hurrying over to the corner of the cellar pounced upon Jack's pumpkin.

"Oh Jack, we've been so worried about you," said the little boy, holding the head tightly in both arms, "but now we'll soon fix you up and fly to the Emerald City, for Snif has grown big again and we've all escaped from the tower."

"So I see," observed Jack as Peter held his head toward the others. "And I'm very glad they chopped off my head and not yours, Peter, for yours would not so easily be put back, and it's lucky they did chop it off too, for otherwise I would never have learned of the forbidden flagon."

"Forbidden flagon!" exclaimed Peter, sitting down on an overturned keg and staring earnestly down at Jack's head. "What has that to do with us?"

"Everything," confided Jack mysteriously. "Has Mogodore started for the Emerald City?" Peter nodded and Snif and Belfaygor both drew nearer, while the little boy explained how they had escaped and how they were now about to fly to the capitol to warn Ozma of Mogodore's wicked intentions.

"But we must not go without that flagon," insisted Jack, after listening attentively to Peter's recital. "Listen: as I was lying here a while ago, hoping that no rats would come to gnaw my fine features, or make a nest in my head, an armed guard came creeping up that ladder you see over in the darkest corner. As he did, another came sliding down from above, and stopping under the lantern they began to converse.

" 'What a bitter waste of time it is, guarding this foolish flagon,' fumed the guard who had climbed the ladder. 'Who ever could find their way to the enchanted cavern through the lost labyrinth, anyway?'

" 'Only one as knows the tricks,' grinned the fellow who had come down to relieve him. 'Left turn left, and always left, and as for the enchanted cavern itself. Bah, what a joke! But have you heard the latest news Do-ab? Mogodore has gone to capture the Emerald City and make himself a King.'

" 'A King,' roared the second, 'Ha! Ha! 'Tis well those foolish folk at the capitol know nothing of this flask. One tip of that forbidden flagon and—' "

"What?" demanded Peter, who had been listening breathlessly to Jack's story.

"Well," admitted the Pumpkinhead regretfully," he didn't say, "but from the nudge he gave his comrade, I imagine there's something in that flask to destroy Mogodore's power."

"But we have the sack, and the Wizard and Ozma have plenty of magic," objected Peter impatiently. "I don't think we'd better stop to hunt for it, Jack. We had better go on to the Emerald City just as fast as we can."

"We had the sack before and Mogodore captured us. Don't forget that," sighed the Pumpkinhead gloomily. "What's happened before may easily happen again."

"It will not take longer than an hour to fly to the capitol, and Mogodore riding at his best speed cannot reach there until afternoon. Perhaps we had better find this flagon, Peter, and make sure of victory this time," murmured Snif thoughtfully, and as Belfaygor sided with the Iffin, Peter rather reluctantly agreed to descend into the enchanted cavern.

"We may lose our way in the labyrinth," said Peter looking down the ladder without much enthusiasm.

"Not while I have my whiskers," smiled Belfaygor, stroking his famous beard, "We'll let them grow along with us and then we'll follow them back."

> "If it weren't for those whiskers
> We'd never be here!
> Hurrah for your beard!
> Three hurrahs and a cheer!"

roared Snif, saluting the baron with his front paw.

"Not so loud! Not so loud!" begged Belfaygor, looking around nervously. "Someone might hear you."

"Do you want to come with us?" asked Peter, looking doubtfully at the Pumpkinhead.

"Better leave me here," advised Jack seriously. "You'll need both hands to fight the guard. "Now don't forget, when you are in the labyrinth turn left and keep turning left."

"And you're sure you'll be all right?" asked Peter, placing Jack's head gently on the cellar floor.

"I certainly cannot be all right if I'm left, but I'd rather be left than right this time," muttered Jack to himself, as his three friends disappeared down the ladder into the labyrinth.

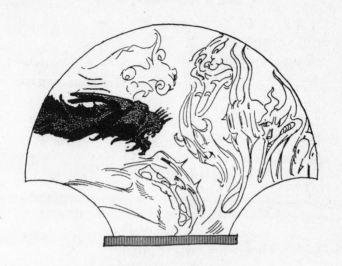

CHAPTER 13

The Enchanted Cavern

"THIS is about as exciting as rice pudding without any raisins," said Peter, treading closely after Snif. For five minutes they had been trudging solemnly through the labyrinth at the foot of the ladder. Every few rods the chilly tunnel would branch off into three or more tunnels, but Belfaygor, always taking the left turn, marched hopefully onward, his red beard trailing like a long and lively vine behind him.

"Are you sure we've been turning left all the

time," asked Peter, after five more minutes of this weary winding. "We don't seem to be getting anywhere at all." Belfaygor nodded emphatically and taking another left turn, gave a sharp exclamation of surprise and dismay. Coming quickly around the bend, Peter and Snif saw that they had reached the enchanted cavern itself.

"Horrors!" shuddered Peter, catching hold of Snif's mane.

"You're right," wheezed the Iffin, rearing up on his hind legs. "Open the sack! Open the sack! These are worse than Scares!" The enchanted cavern was small and dim and lit only by a flickering red light, but ranged around the walls was such a company of Ugly Muglies that Peter's fingers, fumbling with the strings of the pirate's sack, shook so he could hardly untie the knots. He finally did get the cord unfastened and opening the sack he advanced a step into the cave. As he did, the Ugly Muglies advanced a step toward him and in a panic Peter realized that the sack was not going to swallow them. Belfaygor turning to run, tripped over his whiskers and fell flat. Peter looked round desperately for a rock or stone to fight with, but Snif, muttering dreadful denunciations in the Grif language, hurled himself bodily at the enemy. There was a dull thud as Snif met the enemy, and next instant he lay stretched on the floor. Peter was almost afraid to look, but forced himself to move forward.

"Come away," begged the little boy in a hoarse whisper, trying at the same time to tug the Iffin to his feet. "Hurry Hurry! Here they come again."

"Again," moaned Snif, opening one eye, "they were never there at all."

"But I see them," insisted Peter. "What knocked you down?"

Instead of answering, Snif lurched to his feet.

"Myself," panted the Iffin, planting his claw in the middle of a red monster's nose. "The walls of this cave are mirrors, boy, magic mirrors. They multiplied us fifty times and in fifty frightful ways. There's nobody here but us." Rubbing his eyes, Peter looked again, then, tip-toeing forward, touched the walls of the cavern. Just as Snif said, they were mirrors, and remembering how he had often laughed at his distorted reflection in the mirror maze at Willow Grove, Peter began to laugh now.

"No wonder the sack wouldn't work," said Peter, jerking the cords tight and tossing the sack over his shoulder. "But it's a pretty good trick at that. Look at me. I'm enough to frighten my own grandfather."

"Oh, come on," grumbled Belfaygor, who was vexed to think he had been so easily scared. "Let's find this miserable flagon and begone. It's stifling in here."

The scowling reflections cast by the mirrors were so confusing, they had to go slowly and carefully, but after circling the cavern several times, they discovered an opening into a still smaller cave. Peter went first, and poking his head under the arch between the caves saw the guard Jack had mentioned, asleep beside a fountain of fire. The fire fountain jetted up from the center of a deep green grotto and in the middle of the fountain, Peter could just make out a small black flagon. With a little cry of triumph he darted into the rocky room.

"You'll burn yourself," puffed Belfaygor, as Peter leaned forward to snatch the flagon from the flames. At his cry of warning, the guard awakened and with spear upraised sprang to his feet. But Belfaygor was ready for him. Seizing his spear, Belfaygor ran 'round the startled soldier, till he was wound up like a mummy in the baron's red beard. Calmly cutting off his end of the whiskers, Belfaygor dragged the helpless guard out of the way. "Let us get this flagon and depart," cried the baron.

"Maybe this fire isn't real," suggested Peter. "Maybe it's a trick like the mirrors." Taking a piece of paper from his pocket, Peter tossed it into the fountain. But it caught fire at once and burned up with such a snap and crackle the three friends jumped back in a hurry.

"I don't mind singeing a few feathers for the cause," said Snif, as Peter and Belfaygor looked longingly at the strange black flask.

"No you don't," said Peter firmly. "You've done your share." With a little smile he touched the lump Snif had raised on his head when he ran into the walls of the cave. "You discovered the mirrors, Belfaygor captured the guard. Now it's my turn." While Snif grumbled his disapproval and the baron stroked his beard uneasily, Peter gazed into the sparkling fountain of fire. Then with a sudden snap of his fingers, he seized Belfaygor's shears, and clipped a long piece from the Baron's red and ever ready whiskers. "Now," said Peter, "you take one end, and I'll take the other." Looking much mystified, Belfaygor did as he was told. They were standing in back of the fire fountain and one on each side. At a signal from Peter both rushed forward. The baron's beard, passing through the flames, knocked the flagon from its stand, before it went up in smoke and the flagon itself rolled into a dark corner of the green grotto. "Wait till it cools off," warned Peter as Snif made a pounce at the flask.

"Gee, I do wonder what's in it and why it's hidden down here?" Impatiently they looked down at the smoking black bottle and after what seemed to be hours, Peter, covering his hand with his handkerchief, ventured to pick it up. It was still smoking hot, but by changing hands frequently, Peter managed to hold it and read aloud the curious legend on the red label.

"The Forbidden Flagon,
To be guarded by each successive
Baron of Baffleburg.
Who breaks the seal upon this flask
Or spills its contents red,

THE FLAGON ROLLED INTO A DARK CORNER OF THE GROTTO.

Brings woe to Baffleburg and dire
Disaster on his head."

"Now that's nice," said the Iffin, wiggling
his nose very fast. "We break the flask to
subdue Mogodore and bring a disaster on our
heads. Don't drop it lad, whatever you do, don't
drop it. I'd like to have a few more geraniums
and see a few more sunsets before a disaster
hits me."

"It is my place to break the seal," announced
Belfaygor in a determined voice. "Give me the
flagon. What care I for disaster if Shirley
Sunshine is saved?"

Peter was really alarmed at the threatening
tone of the red verses. "Not now, Belfaygor,
wait till we reach the Emerald City and then
maybe we won't have to break it at all."

"That's the talk," said Snif, waving his tail
gently to and fro. "Come, let's start back."

Peter tucked the flagon into his pocket.
"We'll go right away," he said. Leaving the
guard still swathed in whiskers, the three
friends stepped from the small cavern into the
large cavern and from the large cavern into the
labyrinth.

Going back they turned right and kept turning
right, but it was slow and tedious and seemed
much longer than before. At last, dusty and
weary, they came to the end and climbed the
ladder into the cellarway.

"Thank the stars, you're here!" cried Jack's Pumpkinhead.

"Not the stars," wheezed Snif, heaving himself up the ladder and dropping heavily on the cellar floor, "not stars, whiskers!"

> "They lead us down, they lead us back;
>   They tied the guard up fast;
> They pulled the flagon from the flames,
>   Long may they wave and last!"

"They have been pretty useful," admitted Belfaygor, giving his beard a thoughtful stroke before he cut it off short.

"Useful," rumbled the Iffin, raising one claw. "They're wonderful. I'm positively attached to them."

"Not half so much as I am," smiled the baron, with another quick clip.

"So you found the flagon," said Jack, as Peter picked up his head and started up the long steep slideway. Peter nodded and with what breath he had left told Jack all about the enchanted cavern and the inscription on the magic flask. There was a rail beside the slide and by holding on to this they managed to pull themselves up without slipping backward. But they were now so impatient to be off that the slide seemed simply endless. Finally they reached the top and hurried down the hallway leading into Mogodore's room of state.

"Here's somebody you'll be glad to see," chuckled Peter, pointing to the stiff figure seated in the chair.

"Some body!" exclaimed Jack's head as Peter held it up. "Why it's mine. Reunite us at once, my boy. Oh, how I have missed me!" It was the matter of but a moment to place the pumpkin head back on its peg. At once Jack arose to his feet and executed a lively jig, in which the Iffin, with more gusto than grace joined him, while Peter and the baron looked amusedly on. The search for the flagon had taken just an hour, and feeling well repaid for their trouble the four valorous rescuers prepared to leave the palace. Jack took out the famous dinner bell to see that it was safe, Belfaygor gave his beard a last cheerful clip, Snif ate the tops of a pot of geraniums and Peter, putting the flagon in his pocket and tightening his hold on the pirate's sack felt ready for any adventure. But as he prepared to jump upon Snif's back, there came a sudden splutter, screech and roar.

"Stop!" screamed a threatening voice. "Stop! Or you shall be boiled like eggs, stewed like prunes, fried like fish." Snif swallowed a geranium whole, Jack's knees knocked together and bent outward, and in spite of himself, Peter clutched at a chair for support.

"Who speaks?" boomed Belfaygor, snatching a sword from the wall and swinging about like a tee-too-tum.

"Die!" thundered the voice again. "Die, you knaves!"

Trembling a little, Peter looked all around but could see no one. As the dreadful threats kept up, Belfaygor went to look behind a screen. but one of Mogodore's hunting dogs, rising from its place by the fire, moved majestically across the floor, picked up a small red box in its teeth, and with an impatient grunt dropped it at Peter's feet. Then with a satisfied yawn, the great dog rubbed against his knee and returning to its post immediately dozed off again.

"It's the sauce box," cried Peter with a gasp of relief. Closing the lid, he smiled cheerfully at the Iffin.

"I'd like to smash its lid," grunted Snif vindictively. "I nearly choked on that geranium."

"Don't do that," advised Jack, leaning down to straighten his knee joints. "Take it along. What frightened us may easily frighten others."

"That's so," laughed Peter, helping Jack to mount Snif's back. "Well, we surely have enough magic now. A dinner bell, a forbidden flagon, a magic sack and sauce box."

"Don't forget Belfaygor's beard," said Snif slyly, as Peter climbed up behind Jack.

"I wish I could forget it," sighed the baron, seating himself next to Peter.

"Oh, well," Peter reminded him cheerfully, "it won't be very long now, Belfaygor!"

"No, not if he keeps cutting it," said Jack calmly.

"I mean it won't be long before we reach the Emerald City," laughed Peter, as the Iffin raised his mighty wings and swooped out the wide open castle doors. "Here we go!"

CHAPTER 14

High Times in Swing City

"AS SOON as we see Mogodore, I'll open the pirate's sack, no fooling!" declared Peter, looking down at the whirling red landscape. Like tiny toys under a Christmas tree, the villages and towns spread out below, and some country people dancing about a May pole looked no larger than dolls.

"Swallowing's too good for him," objected Belfaygor, stroking the sword he had taken from the castle hall. "Let me have one good swing at him—one good thrust, before you open that sack!"

"If we trust to a thrust, we may all be undone,
'Tis better to sack him than whack him, my son!"

called Snif, looking over his shoulder to wink at Peter.

"Much better," approved Jack Pumpkinhead. "Let us open the sack, break the forbidden flagon and throw the sauce box at his head."

"Yes, and bring a dire disaster on our own," said Peter, remembering the warning on the magic flask. "We'll give the flagon to Ozma and let the Wizard of Oz decide what is to be done with it."

"Well, I hope he can do something with my beard," groaned Belfaygor, looking ruefully at the blisters on his thumbs. "I cannot keep on cutting it forever. Besides it will frighten the Princess."

"He'll fix it," promised Peter confidently. "The Wizard of Oz can fix anything. Oh boy, I can hardly wait to see them all again. Is Scraps as funny as ever and has Kuma Party visited the Emerald City since I left?"

"He lent Ozma a hand just the other day," said Jack, throwing both arms around Snif's neck, as he made a sudden dive through a cloud. "She was having trouble with the Hammerheads and needed a strong hand to subdue them." Peter had met Kuma Party on

his first journey to Oz. This singular gentleman can really send his hands, feet, head or body wheresoever he wishes. Belfaygor listened politely, as Peter told how Kuma's hand had guided him to the Kingdom of Patch, helped him escape, and how it had afterward arrived at the Emerald City in time to catch the Gnome King.

"If we had it now, we could send it down for some apples," sighed the little boy, peering hungrily over the Iffin's wing. Snif was flying low, to be sure not to miss Mogodore, and the orchards, laden with rosy red fruit, looked tempting indeed.

"Why not order lunch," asked Jack, as Peter continued to gaze longingly at the apples. "Eat as you fly!"

"Why not?" chuckled Belfaygor, slipping his shears into the pocket of his coat. "I could make some food fly right now." As Peter was wondering just how they would manage the trays, Jack rang and up beside the Iffin flashed the faithful slave of the bell. But he did not

151

carry the tray this time. It was borne by Biggen, Mogodore's bodyguard, and the great fellow trod clumsily through the air, his eyes rolling with fright and fury. At a haughty gesture from the slave, he set the tray on Peter's lap. Then raising his fist, he was about to pound Peter on the head, when the little black seized him by the coat-tails and both disappeared.

"Wh—ew," whistled Peter ducking his head, "what do you think of that? Look out, here comes the other one!" As Jack rang the bell again, Little, just as angry as Biggen, came hurling toward them with the baron's dinner. The slave winked mischievously at Peter as the enraged bodyguard placed the tray on Belfaygor's knees; then catching the surly fellow by the ear, he vanished before Little could do any harm.

"Good enough," roared Snif, who had witnessed the whole proceeding over his shoulder. "What sweet little sprites they do make.

> "If Mogodore could see them skipping lightly
>   through the sky,
> He'd shiver in his great red boots, and shake
>   like custard pie."

"That's what we have for dessert," said Peter, lifting the cover off his tray. "Say, it's too bad you don't eat pie, Snif."

"Or roast guinea," murmured Belfaygor, between rapturous bites. "I'll give you three horses and a couple of hunting dogs for that bell, Peter."

Peter smiled to himself, for he could not help thinking how crowded three horses and a dog would make the small back yard at home. But he tactfully said nothing, for he had decided to present the magic dinner bell to Ozma. Enjoying the Red Jinn's delicious dinner, looking dreamily down at the lovely mountain scenery beneath, Peter concluded that this was even more exciting and interesting than eating on the train.

"I shall think nothing of airplane trips after this," mused the little boy, sipping his chocolate complacently. "I don't believe anything could ever surprise or frighten me again; not even a highwayman." Finishing off his pie, Peter closed his eyes and was fighting an imaginary duel with a Mexican bandit, when he was suddenly seized by the shoulders, jerked from the Iffin's back and hurled like a ball through the air. His first thought was that Biggen, returning for the magic tray, had taken this means of revenge, but there was no sign of either bodyguard. In spite of his recent boast, Peter's heart beat with dreadful thumps as he turned over and over in the air. But just as he gave himself up for lost, he was skillfully caught by the ankles.

"Howde-do!" called a pleasant voice, and looking up Peter saw a jolly fellow in silk tights swinging by his heels from a high trapeze. He

wore a crown, which was held in place by ribbons tied beneath his chin. Now hanging head down, if you are not accustomed to it, is terribly upsetting and Peter was too upset to say a word. "Welcome to Swing City," said this strange sovereign in his high, jolly voice. "I am the King and the highest Swinger here. In fact, Hi-Swinger's my name," he coughed self-consciously. "But you must meet the Queen, Tip Toppsy the Tenth!" As he said "Meet the Queen," Hi-Swinger flung Peter carelessly downward. Any desire Peter had ever had to do circus stunts, he lost in that second dizzy drop through space. Fortunately, he did meet the Queen, somewhere in mid air. Like the King she was hanging head down from another swing, and grasping both of Peter's wrists swung him gently to and fro.

"Isn't he perfectly precious," cooed her Highness, smiling amiably down at the little boy. "I hope he'll stay with us always. What lovely hair! What sweet red cheeks. He'll make a perfectly splendid swinger, Highty." Now if there was one thing Peter detested it was being fussed over, and the Queen's speech made him squirm with embarrassment and rage. But before he could do more than mutter, Tip Toppsy swung him back to her husband. "Shall we dress him in pink or blue?" she called anxiously.

"Blue," answered the King, catching Peter and drawing him up close so he could look into his eyes. "But, my dear, see what's coming now. Who is this pomiferous person?" Throwing Peter carelessly aside, the King caught Jack Pumpkinhead, who had just been tossed up by someone below. Peter himself was seized by a smiling trapezist, some twenty feet beneath. Before the fellow could throw him further, Peter pulled himself desperately up on the trapeze, and holding tight to the side rope stared dizzily around. Over his head, and under his feet, pink and blue clad figures swooped and darted like birds. With lightning speed they shot from swing to swing, skipped recklessly across spidery ropes and balanced perilously on swaying cords.

"Trapleased to meet you," murmured the owner of the trapeze, swinging up beside Peter. "Hang around a while. You'll like it. 'Tis an easy life we lead—trapeasy," he added with a sly wink. "Have you met the Queen?"

"Yes! Yes!" shuddered Peter, moving as far from the tumbler as he could. "I'm looking for my friends."

"Is that one of them?" inquired the acrobat, pointing off toward the left. "Ha! Ha! Ha! The tight rope walkers will never let that fellow go. They are great cut-ups, you know, great cut-ups. Why, look at his beard! It's growing longer every minute. They can cut rope after tight rope from it. Ha! Ha! Ha! Rope after rope!"

"No they can't," shouted Peter angrily, "and you'd better be careful. We're wizards, and

will destroy you like that." Letting go of the
side rope with one hand, Peter snapped his
fingers sharply.

"Will you?" said the trapezist in an interested
voice. "Then that means a battle, an acrobattle.
Hello! It's begun already. Look at that old
Nibblywog down there. Come on, we're missing
all the fun!"

Jerking Peter from the swing, the acrobat
hurled him to the next trapeze and the next
and the next, until everything turned topsy-
turvey. Peter could no more have opened the
pirate's sack than he could have counted the
somersaults he took in the air. Jack had long
since lost his head, and Peter could see the
acrobats tossing it about like a ball. Below that
a troupe of tight walkers were dancing merrily
on Belfaygor's beard, which had been stretched
between two swings. The baron himself was
held fast by a dozen swing citizens and Snif,
trying to help first Peter then Belfaygor, was
buffetted and banged with the hard fists of the
aerialists.

"How dare you hold us up in this high
handed manner," roared the Iffin, nearly beside
himself with rage and indignation. There is no
telling how long Peter and his friends would
have been tossed about had not a sudden shake
dislodged Mogodore's sauce box from the little
boy's pocket. Opening as it fell it immediately
filled the air with such a thunder of screams,
threats and brazen screeches, several swing

citizens lost their hold upon the swings and fell trembling through space.

"Magic," squealed Hi-Swinger, clutching his crown with both hands. "Drop them! Drop them at once!" So Peter and his companions were dropped as suddenly as they had been taken up by these fickle folk of the air, and with sickening speed went whizzing downward. Peter was too dizzy to realize he was falling again, and Snif, trying to catch all of them at once succeeded only in rescuing Jack's head as it whirled past. But he need not have worried, for under this strange city a great net was suspended and into this net they all landed with a bounce that promptly sent them skyward again.

"Score one for the sauce box," panted Peter as he fell back. "Gee-whiz—I never want to see another swing as long as I live!"

"Neither do I," muttered Belfaygor, unwinding himself from his long red whiskers and feeling for his shears. Snif said nothing, for he was trying to hold Jack's body steady and place his pumpkin back on its peg. Peter hastened to assist him and soon Jack was himself again.

"Ups and downs," he mused sadly. "Nothing but ups and downs! And how are we to get out of this net, may I ask?"

"I'll cut a hole in the net and we'll drop through," said Belfaygor promptly. "It's not far to the ground!"

"Another fall," groaned Jack, holding his

head with both hands. "Oh, think of something else!"

"If we stay here," said the Iffin, "the Swingers will probably come back and if we don't hurry, we'll miss that rascally baron and he'll capture the Emerald City before we catch him."

"I'll fall," quavered Jack, crawling toward the opening Belfaygor was cutting in the net. "I'll do anything for Ozma!"

"We've certainly done a lot of falling for her so far," sighed Peter, scrambling after Jack. "Let me fall first and then I can help you." Holding for a moment to the edge of the opening, Peter dropped lightly to the ground. Then reaching up he caught Jack under the arms and carefully eased him down. Belfaygor quickly followed Jack and Snif bounced through in short order.

"Well, we've lost the sauce box and a lot of time but we've met a new and curious kind of people," said Peter, pulling down his jacket.

"And so did they," smiled the Iffin, giving himself a shake and examining two places where he had lost some fur. A hurried search proved that the magic bell, the sack and flagon were still in their possession. Jack was no worse for his swinging and though Snif, Peter and Belfaygor still felt dizzy and shaken by their unexpected experiences in Swing City, they decided not to stop and rest but to push straight on for the capitol.

"From now on," said Snif gravely, "we must keep a sharp look out for trouble."

"I'll watch the air," said Jack, seating himself quickly.

"I'll watch the ground," promised Peter, springing up briskly behind him.

"And I'll see that we're not followed," said Belfaygor, climbing on last of all.

"Then off we go," rumbled Snif. "What a lot I shall have to tell my grandchildren, if I ever have any grandchildren. I hope they'll be just like you, Peter," he added with an affectionate glance over his shoulder. Peter smiled faintly to himself, for he did not see how this could be but he was too polite to argue the question, and fixing his eyes upon the road below looked eagerly for some sign of Mogodore and his men.

CHAPTER 15

Peter Opens the Pirate's Sack

"WHAT a curious existence," mused Belfaygor, as Snif came to the end of Swing City's net and soared joyfully into the air. "Well, everybody has his own idea of comfort, but as for me, I prefer a castle with someone to serve the soup and bring on the venison." Snipping off his beard, the baron gave a homesick sigh and looked glumly at the tiny farms and villages below.

"A place where a fellow can keep his feet on

the ground and his head on his shoulders, suits me," declared Jack in a weary voice. "I've never lost my head so often as on this trip. Did you see those savages using it for a ball?"

"They used my beard for a tight rope," said Belfaygor in an exasperated voice, "so what could you expect?"

"And they called Snif a Nibblywog," laughed Peter, "and threw me around like an old shoe. All they need to make them monkeys is tails!"

"Don't insult a monkey," said Snif, looking reprovingly over his wing. "I've known some polite monkeys in my day. But those highwaymen!" Snif gave a disgusted grunt. "I've a notion to fly back and settle with them after this other affair is all over."

"I hope we didn't miss Mogodore while we were being held up there," worried Peter. "It must be nearly four o'clock now and we certainly ought to overtake him soon. Are you sure we are flying in the right direction, Snif?"

"Yes," said the Iffin expertly circling a dark cloud. "Why there he is now!" Flapping both wings violently together, Snif pointed with his claw. "There, coming out of that forest—Mogodore and all his men! See the sun shining on their spears." With a swoop that nearly unseated his riders, the Iffin hurled himself over the wood and the next instant they were hanging motionless over a tossing sea of spears.

"The Princess," cried Belfaygor, leaning far over. "There's Shirley Sunshine riding out ahead. Fly lower, Snif, fly lower and we'll snatch her up and be off!"

"No we won't," muttered the Iffin grimly. "We'll open the sack and catch this kingdom stealer, first. Open the sack, Peter! Open the sack, there's no one to stop you now." So intent upon their purpose were the warriors below, they never saw the red monster above their heads. Now Peter had untied the pirate sack. Now it was ready to open. Seizing Snif's wing to balance himself, Peter stood up in order to hold the sack directly over the enemy. As he did a great gust of wind tore the sack from his hands, filled it full of air and sent it spinning up like a balloon high above their heads.

"Oh," choked the little boy, nearly losing his hold on Snif, "nothing ever happens right. Doggone that sack anyway!"

"The flagon," screamed Jack. "Throw the flagon. Quick before he gets away!"

"I'll do it," whispered Belfaygor eagerly. "Give it to me, Peter. Quick!" Tugging the forbidden flagon from his pocket, Peter was about to pass it to the baron, when a hoarse scream from the Iffin made him pause.

"The sack," panted the red monster, flapping his wings desperately. "It's coming straight for us! Look! Look! Look out! Look up! Hold on!"

"If that comes nearer, we are gone!" Jack took one startled glance upward, and then instead of holding on, snatched the flagon from Peter's hand and dove recklessly to earth. As

he did, and as the last of Mogodore's army galloped out of danger's way, the wretched sack, its mouth wide open came hurling down upon the rescuers. Jack had been wise to jump. Before Peter or the baron could follow him, they were snapped up, I mean down. An ear splitting growl came to Jack as he turned over and over in the air. The fright of vanishing had restored Snif's gu—rrr! And it was a real Griffin, not an Iffin who disappeared into the fathomless depths of the pirate's grab bag. Then floating calmly to the ground, the terrible sack settled calmly against a pink hay stack and was still. Not far away, Jack lay face down on another soft mound of pink hay. So tightly had he held to his head and the flagon, he lost neither during the fall and the hay had saved both from smashing, but when Jack rolled over and started to rise, he found that his left leg had bent under and broken off at the knee. Being of wood, Jack suffered no pain, but it was frightfully inconvenient, and it was now impossible for him to walk, or even hobble. Shaking his fists as the last of Mogodore's riders disappeared in a cloud of dust, Jack sank dejectedly against the hay mound and tried to collect his scattered thoughts. His purpose in plunging from the Iffin's back, had been to break the flagon over Mogodore's head and save the Emerald city at any cost, even if he himself were destroyed. But now it was too late! Mogodore was gone, Peter, Snif and Belfaygor

had vanished and he himself was a broken man.
The wicked Baron of Baffleburg, with none to
stop him, would march boldly to the capitol,
fall upon its unsuspecting inhabitants, enslave
them all and seize the magic treasures for
himself. This dark picture fairly made Jack
groan and when he spied the magic sack resting
against the next hay stack he positively shuddered.

"All that is left of three faithful friends,"
mourned Jack. "I hope there's room for Belfaygor's beard in that bag or they'll all be
smothered. I hope they're not mixed with
Scares. I must get that sack. Whatever happens
I must get that sack and take it to the Wizard
of Oz." At the thought of touching the
enchanted bag, Jack shook like a tree in a hail
storm, but controlling his fear and distaste, he
dragged himself to the haystack. First he pulled
the cords that closed the top, then hanging it
carefully over one shoulder, dragged himself
back. His broken leg and the forbidden flagon

lay side by side in the straw, and raising his voice Jack shouted loudly for help. But the pink hay field was a long way from the farm house and no one heard him except a few curious crows who answered his cries with dismal screeches. Finally Jack grew so hoarse he could shout no more and, holding his head in both hands, he tried to think of some way to reach the Emerald City.

"If the Scarecrow were only here," sighed Jack dolefully, "he would be sure to hit upon some clever plan, "but I am only a poor stupid pumpkin head with only a few dried seeds for brains." Realizing that the whole fate of the Kingdom of Oz depended upon him, poor Jack pressed his head with his wooden hands and thought so hard that the seeds inside skipped about like corn in a corn popper. And one must have been a seed of thought, for presently Jack gave a little bounce and feeling in his pocket drew out the Red Jinn's bell. "I'll make that slave help me," muttered Jack determinedly. Just how the slave could help him Jack did not stop to figure out, but anything was better than sitting foolishly on a haystack while little Ozma was facing capture and possible banishment. So Jack tucked his broken leg under one arm, tightened his hold on the pirate's sack, put the precious flagon in his coat pocket and boldly rang the silver bell.

"I hope he does not bring those meddlesome bodyguards," muttered Jack leaning forward anxiously. The slave of the bell appeared so promptly this time that his tray almost hit Jack in the nose. Placing the tray on Jack's lap the little fellow backed away and was preparing to vanish when Jack sprang to his feet, and scattering dishes in every direction seized the small servitor by the arm.

"Stop," cried Jack Pumpkinhead desperately. "Stop! You must help me." But Jack might as well have tried to stop the wind. With a shrill cry, the Red Jinn's slave vanished. Jack also vanished. Now there was no one in the pink hay field at all. Only a pink rabbit, who wiggled his nose anxiously and then began nibbling at a stalk of celery that had fallen from the magic tray.

CHAPTER 16

In the Palace of the Red Jinn

IN ABOUT three whirls and one spiral Jack
found himself on the steps of a glittering
red glass palace. It stood on the edge of a green
glass sea, whose waves broke with a melodious
tinkle and crash on the beach below. The beach
itself was a gleaming stretch of glass splinters,
most dangerous to the tread of unwary travellers. Jack was so confounded by his sudden
arrival in this strange place that for several

moments he was scarcely aware that the slave of the bell was addressing him.

"Be pleased to enter the castle of the Red Jinn," murmured the little black boy politely, repeating the words till Jack at last did hear him.

"Is the owner of this palace also the owner of the magic dinner bell?" asked Jack uneasily. The slave nodded brightly and after an inquisitive glance at Jack's broken leg which he still carried under his arm, he offered his shoulder to Jack. With his assistance, Jack began hopping doubtfully upward. There were nearly a hundred steps, and moving up and down was a vast and colorful company of turbaned gentlemen, who might have stepped directly from the Arabian Nights. As each one passed he took off his slipper and tapped Jack smartly on the head.

"What, what have I done?" stuttered Jack, trying to protect his head with his arm. "Why do they strike me and why do they smile as they do it?"

"It is the custom in this country to take off the right shoe and tap a visitor upon the head as a polite method of salutation and greeting," explained the slave calmly.

"Greeting," groaned Jack, ducking back to avoid another slipper waver, "well, if we meet many more of your countrymen my head will be a squash instead of a pumpkin. Why can't they shake hands, like we do in Oz?"

"Every country has its own customs," answered the slave stiffly. "Why do you wear such a soft head, pray?"

"Because I'm accustomed to it," replied Jack a little sulkily. "It's the kind of head that goes with my kind of person."

"A turban would help," observed the slave as another citizen greeted Jack boisterously with his slipper.

"I don't need a turban," said Jack, hopping desperately up the last step. "But I do need help. My friends have disappeared into an enchanted sack and my country is in danger of destruction. I must have help. Do you think your master is powerful enough to help me?"

"It depends on how you strike him," murmured the slave indifferently. "There he is now. You might ask him." The glass doors of the palace were wide open, and Jack looked anxiously into the great red glass throne room. The doorways and arches were hung with

strands of strung glass triangles and the musical
tinkle of these strange curtains was both
pleasant and delicate. All of the furnishings
were of sparkling red glass and a double line of
tall vases led directly to the throne. A strange
drowsy incense rose in pink clouds to the
ceiling. At first Jack thought the Jinn was
merely another vase, but as with the black
boy's aid he hopped nearer, he saw that the
vase-like figure on the throne had legs crossed
on the spun glass cushions and hands clasped
round his fat and shiny middle. No head was
visible; nothing but a lid with a round knob on
the top. A sleepy black wielded a great fan
drowsily over this portly person, and Jack after
pausing uncertainly took the leg he still carried
under his arm and tapped the Jinn sharply on
the lid. Instantly it raised up and from the
vase-like interior of this strange sovereign rose
an enormous red head with an exceedingly
pleasant, round face. He blinked curiously at
Jack and then turning to the slave wheezed
good naturedly, "Well, well! Ginger, my boy,
what have you brought me this time? I am
delighted that our bell was stolen. It keeps us
in touch with the outside world and has already
got us two extra slaves. But this one is the best
yet." He looked Jack up and then down. "I
haven't been so amused in a thousand years."

"Don't you want the bell back?" asked Jack,
holding it out uneasily. He had expected the

Jinn to be very angry at the holder of his magic treasure.

"No! No! Keep it and welcome! Just to look at you is worth a hundred dinner bells," said the Jinn, smothering a chuckle behind his fat hand. "An odd enough appearing gentleman, Ginger, is he not? And so polite! Where we but remove the slipper he has taken off the entire leg to do us honor. Tell me, who and what are you, most curious sir?"

"You struck him exactly right," whispered the slave encouragingly. "Speak up and he may help you."

"I am Jack Pumpkinhead, your Majesty," said Jack, balancing himself with great difficulty, "and a simple citizen of Oz."

"I believe you," puffed the Jinn and forthwith broke into such a series of strange sounds that Jack drew back in dismay.

"What language is that?" he asked in a faint voice. "I do not seem to understand your Majesty's remarks." The Red Jinn's lid, which he wore quite jauntily for a hat, was still quivering, but controlling himself with a great effort he wiped his face on a red silk hanky.

" 'Tis the laugh language, Jack," he confided with a wink at the little slave. "The ha, ha, and ho, ho, of great merriment. Do you not speak this language in your country, fellow? The guffaw and the snicker, the giggle and roar of pure hilarity! Ho! Ho! You are doing me good, great good! Come join me in a little roar and we'll speak the laugh language in all its branches."

"But I do not feel like laughing," said Jack wearily. "I have lost my best friends and will lose my country too, if your Highness does not help me. Are you very powerful? Are you important enough to help me?"

"Terribly important," answered the Jinn, pursing up his lips. "At least to myself." He nudged the slave of the bell, who nodded delightedly, and Jack, without further parley, held up the pirate's sack.

"In this bag," said Jack solemnly, "are a little boy, a baron and a flying red monster."

"No?" murmured the Jinn leaning forward incredulously. "How did they get in the bag? How will they get out again and if they stay in an age will they become baggage? Ha! Ha! Ho! Ho!" The Red Jinn's mirth was extremely distressing to poor Jack, but feeling that everything depended upon the wizard's help, he smothered his resentment and patiently told the whole story of his adventures since Peter's arrival in Oz. As he proceeded the Jinn's expression grew more sober and at the conclusion of the story he clapped his hands sharply. Immediately Jack's broken leg snapped back into place, and with a surprised skip, Jack began marching up and down.

"That is the first step toward helping you," smiled the Jinn, holding up his hand to silence Jack's outburst of gratitude. "Now we must find a way to send you to Oz, release the prisoners from the sack and break the forbidden flagon without disaster to yourself. My magic looking-glass would show us where your friends are but not how to rescue them, my magic umbrella would carry you to Oz, but I need that myself. Let me think! Let me think!" Wrinkling his brows, the Red Jinn retired into himself and shut the lid.

"Will he come out again?" asked Jack, turning nervously to the little slave. The slave nodded impressively. So Jack, fixing his eyes earnestly on the Jinn's red lid, waited for him to reappear. And presently his head popped up and with snapping eyes he leaned forward. First he whispered nine words in Jack's carved ear and next, eight more. Then, leaning back, he regarded Jack with a pleased and satisfied smile.

"Now all we have to do is to arrange for your journey to Oz," said the Jinn, tapping his fingers upon the arm of his glass throne. "I believe I'll send you off in my Jinrickasha. Would you like that?"

"Why he's gone," shouted Ginger, leaping into the air. "Gone! Vanished! Departed!"

"So he has," spluttered the Jinn, lurching forward and rubbing his eyes with astonishment.

"Was it by your Majesty's magic?" queried the Slave of the Bell breathlessly.

"Not by my Majesty's magic, but some other meddlesome magic. Hash and horseradish! Now

I shall never hear the end of the story!" Pulling in his head so suddenly that the lid came down with a crash, the Red Jinn dropped back on his cushions, and the little slave, having experienced the extreme of his master's temper when disappointed, tip-toed hurriedly from the royal presence. What had become of our hero? Who had spirited Jack Pumpkinhead away from the palace of the Red Jinn?

CHAPTER 17

The Capture of the Emerald City

IN THAT delightful hour before dinner, when it is too early to go in and light the lamps and too late to go for another picnic or swim, it is a pleasant custom in Ozma's palace to gather in the garden for games. Almost any fine evening at dusk, if you were to peep over the wall of the green castle, you would see all the celebrities and most of the courtiers playing hop scotch or prisoner's base. The ruler of Oz, as most of you know, is a little girl fairy and

The Capture of the Emerald City

Ozma is quite as fond of fun and good times as you are. Dorothy, Betsy and Trot, Ozma's best friends and advisers are little girls too, so that life in the Emerald City is bound to be interesting and gay. And how could it be otherwise, with so many unusual and amusing people living in the palace?

The Scarecrow spends most of his time there, though he has a splendid residence of his own, and for fun and good comradeship there is no one like this jolly straw-stuffed gentleman. He was lifted from a pole and brought to the Emerald City by Dorothy on her first journey to Oz. Dorothy, herself, was blown to Oz in a cyclone and has had so much fun and so many adventures that she would not think of living anywhere else. Betsy and Trot are from the United States, too, but prefer life in the Emerald City to life in America, as indeed I should myself. Almost everybody has heard of Tik Tok, the copper man. Tik Tok is not alive, but very lively and when properly wound can walk, talk and run as well as anybody.

Justly famous is the Tin Woodman. Whole books have been written about him, for Nick Chopper is Emperor of the Winkies and almost any child in Oz can tell you the strange story of Nick and the enchanted ax that chopped off his arms and legs, severed his trunk and finally chopped off his head. After each accident, Nick had himself repaired by a tin smith, till he was entirely a man of tin, and like the Scarecrow he spends more than half his time in the capitol. Then we must not forget Sir Hokus, a real Knight, who was rescued after seven centuries of imprisonment in Pokes. Now where, but in Oz, could a Knight last for seven centuries, and be so spry, so bold and so full of interesting stories? Where, but in Oz, could one find a Wizard able to whisk one about with magic wishing pills and conjure up Ozcream and pop-overs by a mere puff of magic powder?

Another prime favorite in the palace is Scraps. Made from an old patch-work quilt and magically brought to life, Scraps adds a touch of fun and gaiety to all the palace parties, for Scraps is wholly without dignity and can think up verses faster than little boys can think up excuses. The Soldier with the Green Whiskers is a fine fellow, too. He is the whole grand army of Oz, and though not very brave has such a splendid uniform and long shining green beard, just to look at him gives one pleasure and satisfaction. Recently a live statue and a medicine man have come to Ozma's court. The medicine man's chest is a real medicine chest, full of helpful remedies and although no one in the Emerald City ever falls ill Ozma has graciously conferred upon Herby the title of Court Doctor. Add to all of these famous characters the Cowardly Lion, the Hungry Tiger and a dozen other strange pets, fifty or more splendid courtiers and servants and you will have a fair idea of the merry company romping in the garden on this early evening in May.

Dorothy had just won an exciting foot race and sinking into a green hammock called gaily to the Scarecrow, "Let's play blind-man's buff and blind-fold everyone but Betsy Bobbin. Then we'll all try to find her and first one who does shall have three pieces of strawberry short cake!"

"A lot of good that will do me," sighed the Scarecrow, patting his straw stuffed stomach, "but if I win, you shall have my cake, Dorothy."

"You'll never win," teased Betsy, beginning to hop up and down with impatience. "None of you will. Remember now, Wizard, no fair using magic to find me."

"Haven't a bit of magic with me. My black bag's inside," laughed the little Wizard of Oz, fitting a big green handkerchief around his head. In less than a minute, Ozma and everyone in the garden was blindfolded. Even the Cowardly Lion had Dorothy's hair ribbon tied securely over his eyes.

"All ready," called Betsy, and tip-toeing over to an enormous butterfly bush, she climbed into the center and sat still as a mouse. But the others were very far from still. With shouts, screams and little roars of merriment they ran to and fro, bumping into each other and throwing their arms around trees and statues and making so much noise that they never heard the tramp of feet on the other side of the

WITH SHOUTS, SCREAMS, AND LITTLE ROARS OF MERRIMENT, THEY
RAN TO AND FRO.

wall. For Mogodore had at last arrived in the Emerald City, and with a rush and without opposition, captured the famous fairy capitol. At sight of his spearmen, the peaceful inhabitants fled into their houses and slammed windows and doors. Unk Nunkie, a brave old Munchkin who had started on a run to warn the people in the palace, was caught by Bragga, tied up securely and carelessly tossed into a greenberry bush. Shirley Sunshine, who had leaped from her horse for the very same reason, was overtaken and put under guard.

"A fine way to help," muttered Mogodore, shaking his finger at her accusingly. "What were you about Princess?"

"I was anxious to see the castle," stuttered poor Shirley, twisting her handkerchief miserably.

"You'll see it soon enough," promised Mogodore. "Just wait till I've conquered this silly little fairy." About forty paces from the castle itself Mogodore dismounted and called a council of war. Leaving five hundred men to hold the city he took five hundred with him to storm the palace and overcome the famous celebrities whom he had read about so often. Shirley Sunshine was left behind until the fighting should be over. Mogodore and his five hundred picked soldiers marched boldly upon the castle.

"High time for a new King here," sniffed Mogodore scornfully. "A city without defenses!

No army! No guards! What can they expect but capture?"

"There may be an army inside the castle walls," warned Wagarag, jogging wearily along at the baron's elbow. "Before we rush the gates we had better look about a bit and see that everything is safe."

"Very good," grunted Mogodore, taking a pinch of snuff. "You and I will go forward. The others may remain here. My spear tossed into the air will be the signal for them to advance." It was a short walk to the walls of the palace, and hoisting himself with great gasps and puffs the Baron of Baffleburg raised his head cautiously over the top of the wall and looked down into the royal gardens. What he saw astonished him exceedingly, and with a soundless chuckle he dropped to the ground. "The silly dunces are playing a game," whispered Mogodore to his trembling steward. "They're blindfolded and all we have to do is to jump over the wall and seize them."

Tossing his spear into the air, Mogodore waited impatiently for his men and when they came hurrying forward, he raised his hand for silence. "Drop over the wall, one at a time, join in this game of blind-man's buff. Each man take one prisoner and tie him to the nearest tree. When all are taken, I will march into the palace, seize the crown jewels and magic belt and proclaim myself King of Oz. All ready." With only a slight scraping of boots on the stones, Mogodore and his men slipped over the wall and into the garden. Betsy Bobbin, sitting breathlessly in the center of the butterfly bush, became suddenly aware of a change in the gay uproar around her. The joyous shouts and good natured exclamations turned to frightened screams and indignant protests and finally to loud shouts for help.

"What can have happened?" gasped Betsy, poking her head out of the bush. What she saw, as you can well imagine, made her sink back in a faint heap. The garden was swarming with armed warriors and Ozma and all of her friends and courtiers were tied to the trees with gold chains and struggling in vain to free themselves.

"I am the only one left," panted Betsy. "I must try to slip out unnoticed and get the magic belt!" In this famous belt, as most of you know, there is such power that the wearer can transform anyone to any shape at all. "I'll turn them to old shoes and door knobs," sobbed Betsy, with another frightened peek out of the bush. The chances of her reaching the palace were slim indeed and finally she gave up all hope, but she could not help feeling proud of the way Ozma of Oz was conducting herself.

"What does this mean?" demanded the little fairy, tearing the bandage from her eyes and stamping her foot as well as she could with so

"A LITTLE BEAUTY," HE MUMBLED, "FAR PRETTIER THAN SHIRLEY
SUNSHINE."

189

many chains around her ankles. "Who are you and what do you want? Release us at once, or my Wizard and my Army will destroy you!"

"Ho! Ho! ho!" roared Mogodore, looking cheerfully down at the furious Princess. "Hand over the keys of the castle my dear, for you are completely conquered and absolutely captured. I, Mogodore the Mighty and Baron of Baffleburg, am the future King of Oz!"

"I'll crown you with my fist," sputtered Sir Hokus, tugging at his chains till the tree he was tied to rocked as if by a tempest. "I'll thump thee on the bean." (Sir Hokus has picked up a lot of slang from Trot and Betsy Bobbin and mixes it fluently with his knightly conversation).

> "We'll change you to a fritter,
> We'll fry you in a pan,
> You rude uncultured critter——
> Do you call yourself a man?"

yelled Scraps defiantly, and all the other celebrities joined their voices to hers, till the din was so dreadful that even Betsy had to cover her ears. But it had no effect upon Mogodore. Quite calmly he continued to gaze down at Ozma and the longer he looked the broader grew his ugly grin.

"A little beauty," he mumbled half to himself, "prettier far than this Shirley Sunshine. I shall marry Princess Ozma," he shouted, suddenly clapping Wagarag so heartily upon the back that the poor steward's iron pot helmet fell over one eye. "Into the palace, fellow and prepare a feast for the wedding! Farewell for the moment, slaves!"

Shaking his spear at the furiously struggling Ozites, Mogodore tramped off to the palace, followed by two hundred and fifty of his men. The others he left to watch the prisoners, and Betsy continued to crouch uncomfortably in the butterfly bush. As the Baron of Baffleburg strode into the castle, Ozma began to speak quietly and comfortingly to her people.

"For the moment," sighed the little sovereign sadly, "we are overpowered and at the mercy of these rude ruffians. But let us be patient and brave and surely some help will come to us."

"I hope there will be no shooting," quavered the Soldier with the Green Whiskers, trembling so his chains rattled dismally.

"If I only had my black bag," fumed the Wizard, trying desperately to free himself. From the screams and crashes indoors, the anxious company in the garden knew that the servants were being overpowered. Presently a long file of them came out between two lines of Mogodore's men, who marched them to a small summer house and carefully locked them in.

"I hope they don't find the magic belt," breathed Dorothy, wriggling into a more comfortable position and trying to smile reassuringly at the Scarecrow who was tied to the next tree. But even while Dorothy was hoping, out dashed Mogodore waving the belt. His helmet had been removed and Ozma's small emerald crown perched ridiculously upon the top of his head.

"I beg that your Majesty will be careful," cried Wagarag, running anxiously after the excited baron. "Remember that belt is very powerful, very dangerous. Have a care."

"I haven't a care in the world," shouted Mogodore, fastening the belt round his arm, for it would not begin to go 'round his waist. "Am I not a King and about to marry a fairy? Go play marbels, Waggy, and let me alone! I am a King and if I choose can destroy this entire country." And then as Wagarag continued to plead and beg him to be cautious he yelled angrily, "Go, attend to the feast, you meddlesome weasel and leave this magic to me. I shall test the powers of this belt at once. Do you know that I can transform anyone here to anything I wish? Begone, before I turn you to a bone and throw you to the dogs." Now indeed did the helpless Oz folk tremble, and as Wagarag, shaking his head sadly, backed away from his foolish master, Mogodore began to look around the garden for someone to transform. Perhaps, because the Patch-Work Girl was the oddest and most amazing person he had ever seen, his eye rested longest upon her.

"I command this ridiculous maiden to become a bird," called Mogodore in a loud voice. And instantly, Scraps was a bird, an exceedingly scrappy bird, too. Wildly flapping her patchwork wings she quickly disengaged herself from the gold chains that bound her to the tree. Then swooping down upon Mogodore, she snatched Ozma's crown from his head and hurled herself into the air.

"Quick! Quick! Change her back! I knew you'd do something silly," groaned Wagarag, as Mogodore stared dumbly upward. "Now she'll fly off and spread the alarm!"

"You bet I will," screeched the Patchwork Bird, and with an ear-splitting screech she soared over the castle and disappeared.

"I told you something would happen," whispered Ozma, smiling quietly at Dorothy. Now if Mogodore had been more practiced in magic, he would instantly have changed Scraps into a stone and she would have dropped heavily and helplessly to earth. But utterly confused and mortified by the unfortunate outcome of his first transformation, the baron pushed his steward furiously aside, rushed into the castle and slammed both gold doors.

CHAPTER 18

Mogodore Meets More Magic

SOON the fragrance of an appetizing repast began to float out to the unhappy prisoners in the garden. Dusk turned to darkness, lights shone from every room in the palace, and in dreadful suspense and discomfort they waited for Mogodore's next move.

"That robber baron really means to marry you," groaned Trot, who was tied to a tree near Ozma, and as if to confirm her words two spearmen came marching determinedly toward them.

"Her Majesty, Queen Ozma is wanted within," bawled the first man, looking around. "Ozma of Oz, this way please." Immediately the little fairy was released from her chains.

"Never mind," she whispered as Trot burst into tears, "remember, Scraps is free and will find a way to help us."

"She'd better hurry," shivered Dorothy, and with sinking hearts they all saw their little leader marched away between the guards. Well-filled plates were being brought out to the soldiers in the garden, but no refreshment of any kind was offered to the prisoners, nor did Betsy Bobbin, crouched in the center of the butterfly bush, find any opportunity to escape from her hiding place. Inside a great feast was laid in the banquet hall and the rude warriors were already seated and banging on the table with their gold forks and knives. Wagarag, an apron tied hastily over his armor, was super-vising the festivities and Mogodore, seated at the head of the table, without even rising waved Ozma to a place beside him. With a little sigh of despair, Ozma slipped into the green throne chair.

"Your future Lady in Waiting," grunted Mogodore, pointing rudely to Shirley Sunshine, who sat on his other side. "I did truly intend to marry this Princess, but find you so much more charming I have chosen you instead."

"Hurrah for the Queen of Oz and Baffleburg!" yelled the spearmen boisterously. Shirley, under cover of the rattling knives and forks tried to whisper her story to Ozma, but Mogodore's loud roars for food soon put an end to that and, pale with distaste and fright, the two little Princesses sat silent, scarcely touching a mouthful of the food that was unceremoniously dumped upon their plates. With a shudder, Ozma looked around her tidy castle. Mud had been tracked over all the velvet rugs, pictures hung sideways and the floor was strewn with broken vases and plates that spearmen playfully hurled at one another between courses. If Scraps succeeded in reaching the castle of Glinda, the good Sorceress who ruled over the South, Ozma knew this powerful ally would immediately fly to her assistance. With agonized ears, she listened for the wings of Glinda's swan chariot. But time went on and no one came. Now that the hunger of the rough company was appeased, they grew more noisy than ever.

"Call this a battle," wheezed Bragga to Mogodore, "are there to be no hangings, no bon fires, no killings of any kind? You promised us a real war. This is as tame as a taffy pull." Tugging discontentedly at his long mustache, the Captain of the Guard looked sulkily at his chief.

"After the wedding you may kill whom you please," promised Mogodore indifferently, "but now I'm going to have another try at that magic belt."

"Take care! Take care!" bleated Wagarag, from the other end of the banquet hall. "I'll wager you're thinking of that forbidden flagon again."

"Right," boomed the baron, sweeping a dozen plates to the floor with his arm. "And right now, I'm going to transport that flagon to this castle and find out what is in it and why it is forbidden. What will happen if the seal is broken? It cannot harm me now. I am no longer Baron of Baffleburg, but King of OZ—King by right of seizure and conquest."

"You'll not be the lawful King till you marry this Princess," quavered Wagarag, raising a trembling finger and pointing to Ozma.

"The old bone is right," grumbled Bragga. "Why not marry her now and be done with it?"

"Marry her now," echoed all the spearmen, "and let us get on with the killing." Pushing back her chair, Ozma jumped up and glanced desperately around the table. Would no one save her from this robber baron and his band? Mogodore, too, rose to his feet.

"I'm King now, I tell you," he insisted stubbornly, "and I'll marry when I'm ready, but now I am going to end the miserable mystery of the forbidden flagon. I command the forbidden flagon and its guard to appear before me," bellowed Mogodore, staring around defiantly. Scarcely had the sound of his voice died

away before there came a crash and splinter of glass and in through a window back of the baron burst a strange flying figure. It was Jack Pumpkinhead, clasping the precious flagon in one hand and holding to his head with the other; brought all the way from the Red Jinn's palace by the mysterious power of the magic belt. With a hysterical little cry, Ozma rushed forward.

"Jack! Jack!" panted Ozma, "have you come to save us?" Solemnly Jack nodded and before a man at the table could move, he whisked off his head, set it on a chair and then and not till then did he hurl the forbidden flagon straight at the Baron of Baffleburg. How he ever managed to aim so true without his head to help him I have no idea, but with a resounding crack the flagon splintered to bits on Mogodore's nose and a thin red liquid began to pour down his cheeks and drop off his chin.

No longer need Mogodore wonder what would happen, when the seal on the forbidden flask was broken! For what would happen, had happened! Stars! Yes!

CHAPTER 19

The Forbidden Flagon Acts

THE GREAT banquet hall seemed suddenly deserted, and except for faint squeaks and muffled screams quite silent. Shirley Sunshine, hurrying around the table, clasped Ozma's hands and both girls stared in stunned silence at Jack, who was calmly replacing his head.

"Why, where have they gone?" cried Ozma. Then all at once she saw, for tumbling from the chairs, scurrying under tables and vainly

trying to hide themselves, was a host of men no bigger than brownies.

"They're shrunk," shouted Jack delightedly. "Ha there, Mogodore the Mighty, mighty little you are now!" Fuming and raging, the midget baron tried to quiet his frightened retainers, but when Toto, Dorothy's little dog, came bounding through the doorway, he fled igno-miniously and hid behind the hearth broom.

"Good dog, Toto, drive them in the corner," approved Jack and Toto, much as a shepherd dog chases sheep, drove the terrified horde of invaders into a corner and gravely sat down to watch them, snapping at any who tried to escape and snuffing at one and then another most curiously.

"It was the forbidden flagon," explained Jack, as Ozma dropped into a chair and looked in complete bewilderment at the brownie baron and his band. "Is anyone hurt? Did I come in time?"

"Yes! Yes!" sighed Ozma, pushing back her tumbled curls. "But how did you know? Where have you been, Jack dear?"

"Where haven't I been," puffed Jack Pump-kinhead, striding excitedly up and down. "Say, what's that noise? Where is everybody?"

"Oh!" cried Ozma, jumping up hurriedly. "The others are in the garden. We must free them at once." But before Shirley Sunshine, Ozma or Jack were halfway to the door it burst open, and the whole company of courtiers and celebrities came charging into the banquet hall.

"Surrender, villains," bellowed Sir Hokus, glaring around furiously. "Where is that braggart Baron!"

"We'll pull his nose! We'll tweak his ears!
Glinda the Good has come, she's here!"

exulted Scraps, shaking her cotton fists joyfully, for she had been immediately restored to her own cheerful self by the Good Sorceress of the South. Glinda, in her lovely red robe and headdress, peered sternly over Scrap's shoulder, ready to bring her strongest magic into play. Seeing no one in the room but Ozma, Jack and Shirley Sunshine, they all stopped short; then catching sight of Mogodore and his midgets, cowering in the corner, they surged forward in still greater astonishment.

"What happened?" demanded Dorothy, seizing Ozma's hands. "The spearmen in the garden suddenly disappeared. Scraps reached Glinda's castle and Glinda came and released us. But what ever happened in here? How did that monster grow so tiny?"

"Perhaps Jack can tell you," sighed Ozma, who was as puzzled as anyone over the curious occurrences of the last few minutes.

"I can," announced Jack, stepping forward importantly, "but it is a long, long story."

"Then do let's sit down," groaned Trot, for

she was mortally tired from the long stand in the garden.

"Are we saved?" quavered the Cowardly Lion, as the stiff and weary company fell into the chairs so recently vacated by the conquerors of Oz. Jack nodded emphatically.

"Then I will attend to the prisoners," boomed the Soldier with the Green Whiskers, springing out from behind a pillar, and very brave since the enemy had been reduced. Striding over to the corner, he stood over the disconsolate warriors, his gun sternly pointed downward. Now Betsy picked up the magic belt from the floor, where it had fallen when Mogodore shrunk, and fastened it thankfully round Ozma's waist. Scraps set the emerald crown upon her curly head, and with great gentleness and ceremony the Scarecrow and Tin Woodman conducted the little ruler to her rightful place at the head of the table. Then the Scarecrow ran out to release the servants, who were locked up in the summer house, the Wizard ran to see if his black bag was safe, Trot wound up Tik Tok, who was completely run down by his terrible experiences, and everybody settled back expectantly to hear what Jack Pumpkinhead had to say.

"Now tell us exactly what happened," begged Betsy Bobbin, as the Scarecrow and all the servants came marching into the dining hall and the Wizard, tightly clutching his black bag, slipped into a seat beside Dorothy.

"Well," said Jack, with a dignified little cough, "before I begin to tell you that, there is something I must do and three brave comrades to be released from an enchantment. The advice of my friend, the Red Jinn, worked once and I shall therefore try it again."

"Before he speaks he must act," chuckled the Scarecrow, who had completely recovered his good humor. "Well, my boy, actions speak louder than words." Leaning on both elbows, the Scarecrow looked on with great interest as Jack snatched the pirate sack from his shoulder, turned it inside out and gave it three quick shakes.

CHAPTER 20

The Wedding Feast

"IS IT a nightmare?" shivered Betsy, clutching Trot's arm, "or a Hallowe'en party? Am I really here, and are they?" And well might she ask, for the last shake of the pirate's sack had filled the room with Fraid Cats and Scares. Screaming, groaning, snatching at one another and the Oz folk, the Scares swarmed this way and that, until the confusion was terrible.

"Actions speak louder than words," mumbled the Scarecrow. "Well, I do not like their actions at all. Call these comrades, friend Jack? Help!

208

Begone! Away with you!" Jumping up the Scarecrow waved his napkin wildly around his head, and all the others, hastily pushing back their chairs, rushed to the assistance of Ozma, who was completely surrounded by the ugly intruders. Jack Pumpkinhead was so stunned and startled by this unexpected happening that he stood perfectly still. Then, resolved to go through with the matter, he shook the sack three times more and this time with the desired result.

"Why it's Peter!" roared Sir Hokus, disentangling himself from ten Scares and hurrying over to the little boy who had just tumbled out of the sack. "Peter, the pitcher—and—" Thumping Scares both left and right, the Good Knight looked doubtfully at the Iffin and Belfaygor, who had rolled out of the bag after Peter himself. "Who are these?" muttered Sir Hokus, making ready to whack the great red monster if it showed signs of attack.

"Don't mind us," begged the Iffin, glaring around the banquet hall. "Keep working! Keep working. I'll help you!" And help he did, with teeth, tail and claw.

"Where am I? How did I get here? How did they get here?" muttered Peter, rubbing his eyes dizzily and trying to collect himself, for he remembered nothing since he had been swallowed by the sack. But he soon recovered, and fighting his way through the frenzied crowd till he reached Ozma's side, cried excitedly. "They're Scares, your Highness. Quick! Send them back to Scare City, before they break everything to pieces!" Glinda and the Wizard had already started an incantation to rid the castle of the horrible horde, but before it was half spoken, Ozma, without waiting for Peter to explain, arose and in a slightly trembling voice called, "I command these people and creatures to return to Scare City at once." And at once, and all together they did. And now straightening their collars and settling their ties, for the encounter had been rough and furious, the Oz folk gazed at Peter and his comrades as curiously as they had gazed upon their pigmy conquerors and the unlovely citizens of Scare City.

"If someone will just explain," said Ozma. "Everything's so terribly mixed up."

"If someone doesn't explain, I shall burst," declared Betsy Bobbin, bouncing out of her chair. "Have you come back to stay, Peter dear, and who are these others?" Peter was a bit breathless and confused himself and looked anxiously around for the baron. But Belfaygor had slipped off unnoticed with Shirley Sunshine.

"Well this," began Peter, placing his hand on the red monster's head, "this is Snif, an Iffin, I mean a Griffin."

> "If Snif's an Iffin or a Griffin,
> I s'pose at us he'd soon be sniffin!"

ventured Scraps, putting her finger in the corner of her mouth.

> "If I should snif at folks so kind,
> I'd be most rude and unrefined."

replied the Iffin, with a wink at the Patchwork Girl, and this little exchange of verses relieved the strain that the whole company had been under.

"Shall I tell the story, or will you?" whispered Jack Pumpkinhead, stepping closer to Peter.

"You," begged Peter, staring with round eyes at Mogodore and his little men.

"They've been eating shrinking violets," muttered the Iffin, rubbing his eyes with one paw and staring even harder than Peter.

"No, it was the flagon," explained Jack, "the forbidden flagon reduced them to midgets. But what became of Belfaygor's beard!"

"It disappeared into the magic sack," grinned Belfaygor, coming into the room at that moment with the little Princess on his arm. "And glad I am that it's gone. I'll never wear another beard as long as I live."

"Beard," put in the Soldier with the Green Whiskers eagerly, "did you have a beard as long and splendid as mine?"

"Did I!" groaned the baron, rolling his eyes to the ceiling. "Ask Peter!" Taking another look at the Soldier with Green Whiskers, he shuddered and turned away. "You remind me of something I'm trying to forget," said Belfaygor.

Now all of this only served to increase the interest and curiosity of the already curious company. "Tell us! Tell us!" cried Dorothy impatiently. So, after Belfaygor and Shirley Sunshine had been properly introduced, Jack Pumpkinhead began the strange story of their journey from Scare City to Baffleburg and from Baffleburg to Swing City and his own transportation to the capitol. And while he spoke, the footmen and other servants moved quietly about, sweeping up broken glass, clearing away the table and removing all traces of the rude baron's short reign in the palace. Guarded over by Toto and the Soldier with Green Whiskers, Mogodore and his men crouched miserably together, wondering what would become of them. Being merciless themselves, they expected no mercy from their captors. In small hoarse voices, they berated Mogodore for meddling with the forbidden flagon and bitterly denounced him for the terrible misfortune that had overtaken them. The rest of the midgets had been discovered and marched in from the garden and soon after word had been sent out through the city that the baron was captured, Unc Nunkie and his nephew Ojo arrived, driving the rest of the baron's tiny warriors and horses before them, so that the entire army were now rounded up in the corner of the banquet hall. But so intent was the company upon Jack's amazing story they scarcely heard the grumbling and complaining of the little men or the frightened neighs of the toy-size steeds.

In the kitchen another banquet was soon under way, more and more candles were lighted and soon the castle began to reflect its old time cheer and friendliness. Little gasps and exclamations of astonishment punctuated Jack's recital and he had to tell over and over how they had escaped from Baffleburg, how Snif had dwindled down when he ate the shrinking violets; how Belfaygor's enchanted beard had helped them out of difficulty and how the mischievous pirate sack had swallowed three of the company, when they were needed most of all. Peter, Belfaygor and Snif were as interested as the others in Jack's visit to the Red Jinn and in the advice that jolly wizard had given.

"You remember the label on the forbidden flagon said that whoever broke the seal would bring a disaster upon his own head?" said Jack, turning to his comrades. Peter and the baron both nodded and Snif waved his tail to show he remembered, too.

"Well," smiled Jack, "the Red Jinn told me to remove my head before throwing the flagon and thus avoid the disaster."

"So that's why you took off your pumpkin," murmured Ozma, who had been puzzled by this strange action of Jack's.

"And he also told me that to release the prisoners from the pirate sack, I must turn it inside out and shake it three times," went on Jack impressively. "So when Mogodore transported me suddenly to the palace, I did both of these things."

"You certainly did," agreed the Scarecrow, shaking his finger at Jack Pumpkinhead, "and brought a horde of horrors about our ears."

"I forgot about the Scares," admitted Jack apologetically, "but they're back where they belong, now, and everything has turned out for the best."

"It certainly has," exclaimed Ozma, jumping up impulsively. "You and Peter, Snif and this brave baron have saved the Kingdom of Oz!" Jack was so overcome by these words that he lost his balance and sat down. But he was quickly pulled to his feet, and next instant the rafters rang with rousing cheers for the four valiant rescuers.

"I wish my grandchildren could hear this," sighed the Iffin, resting his chin on one claw.

"Oh! Have you grandchildren?" asked Ozma, leaning forward politely.

"No," murmured the Iffin in an embarrassed voice, "but I may have. And they'll be interested to hear about this."

"Take my advice and never have any grand-children," whispered the Scarecrow confidentially. "I'm a grandfather, and I know." Before he had time to explain what he meant, two footmen came grandly forward to announce that dinner was ready, and no one, I assure you, was sorry for that.

"I know what to do," cried Dorothy as the green coated servitors began marching in with trays of savory meats and vegetables. "Let this be a wedding feast for Belfaygor and Shirley Sunshine."

"Hurray for a wedding feast," shouted the

Iffin. "Grr—rah!" forgetting he had recovered his growl, the red monster let out such a terrific roar that the Cowardly Lion swooned away and had to be revived with a jug of cider. But he soon recovered and a wedding feast it was and fit for a royal bride, I do assure you. Snif had eight geranium plants and an Easter lily and was happier than he had ever been in his whole fabulous existence. Never in the history of Oz was there a merrier banquet nor a happier crowd. Delighted to have Peter with them again, the Oz folk forgot their recent capture and had such a time as only those dear and delightful folk can have. Jack Pumpkinhead insisted upon being lit up for the celebration, so he was. Snif and Scraps kept the company in gales of laughter with their rollicking rhymes and when the wedding was solemnized by the highest judge in Ozma's court, Belfaygor and his bride were toasted in tall tumblers of Ozade and simply showered with emeralds and quickly gathered gifts of every sort and description.

"What did it feel like to disappear into that sack?" asked Trot, in a little pause following the wedding.

"Well, once," said Peter, fixing his eyes thoughtfully on the Iffin, "once I had a tooth pulled and took gas. It was like that, Trot. I just went out that's all." At once the others began to recall their own experiences with vanishings and disappearances and not till daybreak did any one think of retiring. Then

the Baron of Baffleburg and his grumbling little
army were locked up in the pantry for safety
and Peter, snuggling down in his emerald
studded bed, decided that this adventure was
even more exciting than the last one.

"I wish I could take Snif back to Philadelphia
with me," sighed the little boy as he finally
dozed off to sleep.

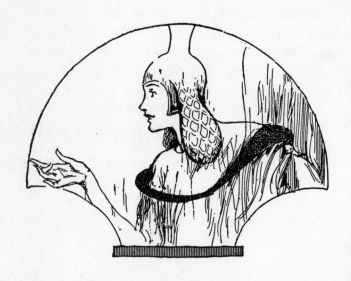

CHAPTER 21

Peter's Return to Philadelphia

NEXT day the festivities continued, and all day long Peter's old chums and acquaintances were calling at the palace, while the celebrities outdid one another to make things pleasant for Belfaygor and his bride. At noon they rode off on the Saw Horse, for the baron was anxious to return to his castle. Peter bade the baron goodbye and promised to pay him a long visit on his next trip to Oz, to ride the horse Belfaygor agreed to keep for him and even wear the armor the baron had promised him as a reward for rescuing the Princess.

Snif spent a happy morning in the royal stable with the famous beasts of Oz and they listened so politely to his experiences he decided to stay on indefinitely at the capitol. The pirate's sack was locked up in the Wizard's strong box and the magic dinner bell stored with the other treasures of the realm, for as Ozma remarked to Dorothy it would be mighty handy for picnics and unexpected visitors. The Fraid Cats and Statues in Scare City were released from their enchantment by the Wizard's long distance magic and Peter and Snif, looking in the magic picture, had the satisfaction of watching them return to their various homes.

"The only thing that still puzzles me," sighed Ozma as they all sat cozily under the trees in the garden late that afternoon, "the only thing that puzzles me is that forbidden flagon. What strange spell could have reduced Mogodore and his followers to midgets?"

"I think I can explain that," answered Glinda, setting her tea cup down on a small green table. "When Scraps flew to my castle yesterday and told of the capture of the Emerald City, I at once turned to my magic record book to discover something about this Baron of Baffleburg. You are all, I am sure, familiar with brownies?" Dorothy and Betsy Bobbin nodded sagely, and all the others quickly inclined their heads. "Well," said Glinda with a wave toward the South, "in the Red Mountains of Oz there are large bands of reddies, who are quite similar to brownies, except for the color of their coats, which are red. To one of these tribes Mogodore and his men really belong. But Mogodore's great grandfather, Jair, was a brave and determined little reddy, whose good deeds and brave actions greatly exceeded his size and strength. So, long ago, a neighboring wizard, whom Jair had done a great service, rewarded Jair by making him and his followers as large in size as they were in deeds and in action. But the enchantment only held so long as the mysterious red liquid remained in the forbidden flagon. Mogodore's father and grandfather guarded the flagon well, but Mogodore knew nothing of its secret power nor of his own ancestry or origin. Being by nature, discontented and greedy he was always puzzling about the strange black flask and at the first opportunity he satisfied his curiosity."

"Well, it's a good thing he did," said Peter, looking thoughtfully at the little band of captives who were being marched up and down one of the garden paths by the Soldier with Green Whiskers. "Now the other barons will have a little peace."

"Let's keep them for toys," proposed Scraps, who was never weary of watching the tiny army.

"No," said Ozma, shaking her head at the Patchwork Girl, "that would be cruel. Has their city grown small too, Glinda?" The sorceress smiled and nodded.

"Then I shall send them back to Baffleburg," declared Ozma, "for they are now too small to harm anyone and there they will be safe and comfortable." As everyone heartily approved of this plan, Ozma touched her magic belt, spoke the few words necessary, and away whisked the bad little baron and his band, to their tiny red city on the rocks.

"Just the same, I wish we could have kept him," sighed Scraps to Dorothy. "He looks so funny when he's mad."

"Hush!" whispered Dorothy, for Peter had risen and in an embarrassed voice was asking Ozma to send him back to Philadelphia.

"Still like baseball better than Oz?" rumbled Sir Hokus, shaking a teasing finger at Peter.

"Well," admitted the little boy, blushing a bit at the question, "the fellows sorta depend on me, Hokus, and then you know there's my grandfather."

"Of course," smiled Ozma, "of course there is. Goodbye, dear Peter, come back soon and as often as you will."

"Goodbye," sobbed the Iffin, overcome at the thought of losing his chum. "If you were my own grandchild, I couldn't love you any better."

"Goodbye!" called Jack Pumpkinhead and

Scraps and all the others and before their gay voices had quite died away, Peter was standing in the dim library of his own house.

"Oh grandfather," cried Peter, "I've been to Oz again and flying is grand, grandfather!"

"Then we must try it some time," observed the old gentleman calmly, and saying nothing at all about Peter's strange absence.

"Oh, may we?" Peter dropped on the arm of the big chair. "May we, really?"

"Well, why not?" demanded grandfather, glancing around the room belligerently and letting his specs fall the full length of the black cord. "Why not? 'Tis a free country and flying's no crime."

"Hurrah!" shouted Peter, bouncing off the chair arm and right that instant he decided that even in Oz there was no better chum nor braver adventurer than this grandfather of his so straightway he told him all that had happened in Baffleburg and other places—indeed all of this story that I have just told to you.

222

THE INTERNATIONAL WIZARD OF OZ CLUB

The International Wizard of Oz Club was founded in 1957 to bring together all those interested in Oz, its authors and illustrators, film and stage adaptations, toys and games, and associated memorabilia. From a charter group of 16, the club has grown until today it has over 1800 members of all ages throughout the world. Its magazine, *The Baum Bugle*, first appeared in June 1957 and has been published continuously ever since. The *Bugle* appears three times a year and specializes in popular and scholarly articles about Oz and its creators, biographical and critical studies, first edition checklists, research into the people and places within the Oz books, etc. The magazine is illustrated with rare photographs and drawings, and the covers are in full color. The Oz Club also publishes a number of other Oz-associated items, including full-color maps; an annual collection of original Oz stories; books; and essays.

Each year, the Oz Club sponsors conventions in different areas of the United States. These gatherings feature displays of rare Oz and Baum material, an Oz quiz, showings of Oz films, an auction of hard-to-find Baum and Oz items, much conversation about Oz in all its aspects, and many other activities.

The International Wizard of Oz Club appeals to the serious student and collector of Oz as well as to any reader interested in America's own fairyland. For further information, please send a *long* self-addressed stamped envelope to:

Fred M. Meyer, Executive Secretary
THE INTERNATIONAL WIZARD
OF OZ CLUB
Box 95
Kinderhook, IL 62345